ONE MURDER TOO MANY

Kari Underwood, an investigative reporter, becomes involved in a curious double murder which puts her in a killer's crosshairs. With Kari's life in danger, Jason Keane leaves his position in the Sutton CID and returns to America to protect her. Kari is thrilled to have Jason back at her side, but has no idea why she is a target; and as she and Jason renew their problematic relationship, they must solve the mystery before she is killed by her unknown assailant. Betrayal, deceit, blackmail, and a vicious drug cartel all play a part in what could mean the death of both Kari and the man she loves.

TERRELL L. BOWERS

ONE MURDER
TOO MANY

Complete and Unabridged

ULVERSCROFT
Leicester

First published in Great Britain in 2013 by
Robert Hale Limited
London

First Large Print Edition
published 2014
by arrangement with
Robert Hale Limited
London

A catalogue record for this book is available
from the British Library.

ISBN 978–1–4448–1927–4

Published by
F. A. Thorpe (Publishing)
Anstey, Leicestershire

Set by Words & Graphics Ltd.
Anstey, Leicestershire
Printed and bound in Great Britain by
T. J. International Ltd., Padstow, Cornwall

This book is printed on acid-free paper

1

His heart pounded against the walls of his chest like a demented beast trying to escape its cage, and his mouth was too dry to have mustered up a whistle even if it meant saving his life. Knees weak with apprehension and his hands sweating inside the snug-fitting leather gloves, he none the less forced himself to go forward. This was it!

Conserving energy within government buildings meant shutting off most of the lights after the usual business hours. While it saved a few cents on electricity it also meant the security cameras would not capture the movement along a darkened hallway as the wraithlike intruder entered an empty maintenance closet. He used a stowed folding chair as a ladder, so that he could reach up and remove the access hatch in the roof. Sweat formed on his brow as he grunted and strained his muscles to pull himself up into the partition. Once situated, he flipped on a miniature flashlight, stuck it between his teeth, and began to crawl.

Moving with the stealth of a cat burglar, the phantom maneuvered carefully along the space between the office ceilings below and the floor of the next story above, making his way to a particular air vent. One slip of his foot on the railing and he would punch a hole in the square ceiling-tiles. If that happened, he would be discovered and his plan would be ruined.

After crawling along for twenty-five feet, he was able to hear them. The couple were swept away with their passion, each moaning and whispering words of love in the other's ear. He hurried as much as he could, knowing time was short. To earn the reward he sought, he had to act quickly.

Espying the intended vent, he shut off his flashlight and tucked it into his shirt pocket. Using the dim glow from the light within the target room, he eased forward silently, carefully, until he could see through the mesh screen. He adjusted his weight on the roof girders, leaned forward and used his cell phone to capture the action. The camera made a little noise, but two bodies below, entwined in mutual ecstasy, were oblivious to the muffled clicks. They felt secure behind a locked door, after quitting time, and with nearly every office deserted.

Satisfied that he had enough photos for his purpose, the intruder eased back the way he had come.

Once back to the utility room he replaced the access panel, folded and stuck the chair away, then exited into the hallway. There was an alarm at the rear door to the parking garage. However, its safety measures were intended to keep people out. One didn't have to enter a security code to leave the building.

Satisfied with his success, the surreptitious photographer kept his ball cap pulled low and his head down as he walked away from the garage area. Once on the main street he headed for his car, parked several blocks away. As he made the short trek, he mapped out his next move. He would text the pictures to the adulteress, who had thought her romantic rendezvous was a secret, and demand a substantial payment. He snickered under his breath.

'Ah, yes! You're going to pay me well to keep your dirty little secret!'

* * *

Kari Underwood was outraged and sought to defend her article to the managing editor of the *Salt Lake City Sentinel*, Scott Quinn.

'It's all true!' she cried. 'People can't even go into our national parks without having to fear being shot at or chased off by drug dealers. There are fields of marijuana growing

3

any place the plants can survive.'

'I'm sure most of those fields are well away from the usual visiting areas,' Scott countered. 'It's not like you are going to run into a dealer if you go on a picnic with your kids.'

'But it's completely unchecked! The government has even put up warning signs not to go back into the hills to camp. How bad does it have to get before someone takes a stand?'

'It isn't up to us to take that stand! These drug people don't like publicity and they play for keeps.'

'Well, my article is only for information, so people can complain to the proper authorities.'

'I understand your motives, but we can't point a finger at the local gangs.'

'Why not?' she cried. 'Many of them are involved in the drug traffic!'

'Yes, but you have no hard proof linking any of those gangs to the drug cartel,' Scott argued. 'You can't expect me to print a story that is founded on suspicions or an unnamed informant's hunches.'

'I thought that's what a newspaper did, put the truth out there for the people!'

Scott shook his head. 'We have to present the facts to back it up. The only thing we can print is the part about what happened to the one family you interviewed, because they reported the encounter to the police. Stick with the single episode, how they were warned out of the area by two men with guns.'

Kari fumed. 'So we ignore the fact that gangs control many of our city streets and the Columbian cartels are importing drugs and we have dealers growing their own crops on BLM land.'

'The Bureau of Land Management has been contacted and the proper authorities will deal with the situation.'

'I interviewed a policeman with the Gang Control Unit to get some of my information. The cops are completely overwhelmed by the numbers of gangs on our streets. Do you know we have gangs from most every denomination in the city?' She paused to glance at her notes. 'We've got the Belizean Bloods, the Surenos, the Lobos, the Crips, the Hard Corps, the Nortenos, along with Asian and Polynesian gangs, plus the usual skinheads and biker gangs. The police can't begin to keep up with them all.'

'The members on the Gang Control Unit have a strict policy about giving interviews or making statements to the press. How did you manage to acquire this information?'

'One of them is concerned for public safety.'

'It means his job if you print something that can be traced back to him.'

'I won't let that happen,' Kari replied.

'And what would you have us do, Kari?' Scott demanded to know. 'If we were to launch a campaign against the drug dealers and all of the hoods who are running loose, we would likely get a fire bomb through one of our windows.' He grunted at the idea. 'And how would we protect our employees? None of us would be safe.'

'But I only suggested that the people push to organize . . .'

'Organize what?' Scott yelped. 'A vigilante or military operation?' He glowered at her with stern disapproval. 'I'm sorry, Kari, but we are not in business to lead the battle against organized crime, crooked politicians or drug cartels. Our job is to report the news, not take up a dangerous campaign that could get some of us killed. Your job is to write stories I can print.'

Kari sighed, knowing the debate was over. 'All right, Mr. Quinn, I'll cut down on blaming local gangs and stick to the single encounter back in the hills.'

Scott's hard stance softened. 'It isn't that I don't care.' His voice was apologetic. 'I have a wife and kids to worry about too. I don't like the idea of the city being infested by drug pushers and armed thugs, but I must do what is best for the newspaper. I can't risk printing an inflammatory article that could make us a target. There are too many gangs with guns, most of whom know how to make a bomb, and more than a few of those will do whatever it takes to silence their opposition.'

'Yes, sir,' Kari acquiesced. 'I guess I can tone it down.'

'You can mention the possibility of an outside cartel providing drugs to local distributors, as well as the incident with the hikers. But we can't point a finger at one or more gangs in the valley. That's going too far.'

'I suppose half the truth is better than none of the truth.'

'An operational newspaper is better than a burned out building,' Scott countered.

Kari gave a nod of understanding. 'I'll edit the story and send it to your screen.'

Scott gave her a pat on the shoulder and left her cubicle. Dee, her friend from want-ads, approached her desk seconds later. Mother of two grown kids, Dee embodied more the part of a sister — often a teenage sister, one full of mischief and pluck. From the pink hue of her cheeks, it was obvious that the matronly woman had overheard at least part of the editor's lecture.

'Um, would it be inappropriate of me to say *I told you so?*'

'Yes, it most certainly would,' Kari snipped. 'I've been properly reprimanded and put in my place.'

'Scott has a point, kiddo,' Dee said carefully. 'You start making noise against the local gangs and you might very well end up wearing a rubber suit . . . one made out of burning tires.'

'What are you talking about?'

'I used to snuggle up with my hubby and watch *The Shield*. Remember that television series a few years ago about a special unit of cops in LA?'

'I watched part of one episode, but it was much too violent and crude for my taste,' Kari replied.

'Maybe so, but it did portray some of the more sadistic truths concerning drugs and gangs.'

Kari clicked an icon on her computer and her article appeared on the screen. 'I can't go to break right now. I've got to cut out all of the juicy stuff and make this story about as dull as if I was commenting on a reality show.'

'That's scraping sludge from the bottom of the barrel,' Dee acknowledged. 'I'll catch up with you for lunch.'

Kari said OK and got to work on the piece. It was difficult, feeling so strongly about something, yet being helpless to do anything about it. She understood Scott's position. It was the same as the mayor, the governor and every other branch of the media. They didn't seem to care.

Perhaps drugs were too much a part of today's society. There were drugs for everything — weight gain or loss, depression, sleep disorders, kids with too much energy, sex drive, memory, anxiety, and a thousand other ailments. Maybe the public was too stoned on regular pills to concern themselves with illegal drugs.

★ ★ ★

Jason Keane stood quietly in the Sutton cemetery, his arms folded against the damp, frigid morning air. The weather around London today was cool and mostly cloudy. Suddenly, a singular ray of sunshine broke through, as if especially to highlight the headstone at his feet. *Doris Mayfield Keane, Beloved Wife, 1984–2009*, were the words carved into the marker. Etched in one corner was the likeness of an angel, one of Doris's favorite icons.

'I still miss you terribly, darling,' Jason said softly. 'Our life together was so brief that each moment remains a precious memory.'

An elderly couple strolled past. Jason waited until they were out of earshot before continuing:

'I met a rather charming young lady when I visited America, Doris. I think you would like her. She is sincere, with a desire to discover truths, to make a contribution and serve society.' He paused. 'I remember, when you grew weak and we knew your time was short, you told me to find someone special. I couldn't imagine anyone who would ever compare to you. And this girl does not compare with you, because she and you are so very different.

'You were confident, and constantly rushed ahead, in a hurry to do as much living as possible in the time you had. This lady is hesitant and lacks your zest for everyday living. She was hurt deeply by a man and is wary of a new relationship. As for me, I haven't yet recovered from the deep sorrow of not having you in my life. The American and I have that much in common; we are both lonely and nursing broken hearts.'

Jason took a long breath and let it out. 'What I'm saying, Doris, luv, is that I might be ready to try and love again. If that should happen with this girl, I don't know when I will be back here.' He swallowed an emotional lump. 'It's not that I think your spirit is here in this spot, because I've often felt you were watching over my shoulder or standing next to me. Your presence is something I take with me wherever I go.

'But the time may be coming when I can fall in love again. You begged me to not live the rest of my life alone, and it's been very difficult without you. I'll never love you less than I did when you were alive, but I might have room in my heart to love another.'

Jason placed the dozen pink carnations (Doris' favorite flowers) on the grave, bowed his head and said a short prayer. Then he stepped back and whispered, 'I'll always love you, Doris. Goodbye.'

Back at the car, his brother-in-law, Jack Mayfield, started his vehicle moving. The two men were not exactly close friends, because they had seldom shared each other's company, but Jack had always struck Jason as a decent and caring fellow. Jack didn't speak for a short time, allowing Jason to open the conversation. When he remained silent, Jack cleared his throat.

'It's good you visited Doris,' he began. 'I stop by with flowers and tend to her grave about once a month,'

'It's hard, isn't it?' Jason said, 'She was so young and vibrant, so consumed with living every day to the fullest.'

Jack smiled. 'Even as a little girl she was an energetic sort, always smiling and laughing. I was five years older than Doris, yet I loved having her around. Most kids I grew up with hated looking after their little brothers or sisters, but I was never put off by Doris' company, She brightened the world with her vitality and cheery disposition.'

'What amazed me was how she never complained,' Jason recalled. 'So many people, when they have a bit of bad fortune, want to blame someone . . . even God. But Doris wasn't that kind of person. The closest I ever saw her come to self-pity was after one of her chemo treatments. Then her main gripe was not feeling well enough to be outside to tend the flowers in her garden or go for a stroll along the river.'

'She taught us a lesson in how to live and how to face death,' Jack said quietly. 'She was much stronger that way than me.'

As they had each had a say concerning Doris, they grew silent, until Jack came round to the present situation.

'So how's the long-distance romance going with the cracking reporter lady in the States?'

'It's a complex situation.'

'I reckon you would like to share some 'quality time' with her,' Jack mused.

'We talk on the phone each week and exchange letters, but it isn't the same as being together.'

'Then you need to take another Atlantic jaunt to give you both a chance to see if you still get on.'

'Yes,' Jason replied. 'But it'll have to wait until I have enough holiday leave built up to make the trip worth while.'

2

Gloria looked up from her desk as the familiar man entered. He beamed his usual charming smile at her, until he saw the hard set of her jaw and the icy crystals glowing in her eyes.

'What is it?' he asked, pausing hesitantly, rather than approaching her desk.

'Close the door, Mr. Martin,' she said professionally, acutely aware that her secretary's desk was within hearing distance, a few feet inside the next room.

Tony shut the door and then frowned at her. 'Glory, honey,' he said sweetly, moving over to her side. 'What's the matter?'

Gloria turned her computer monitor around so he could see the picture on her screen. Tony sucked in his breath when he realized the photo was of him and Gloria!

'What the hell?!' he howled, both outraged and terrified. 'When . . . ? How could this have happened?'

'Keep your voice down!' Gloria snapped. Then she rose to her feet and began to pace irritably around the room. She wrung her hands for several moments, then stopped to

14

face her clandestine lover.

'These arrived while you were having a good time down at Universal Studios with your family. The blackmailer demanded fifty thousand dollars!' She swore and began to pace once more. 'I paid the money and the blackmailer promised to delete the pictures, but we have to make sure he's telling the truth.'

'Glory, honey!' This time Tony whined. 'We can't let those pictures get out. I've got three kids.'

'I *know* you've got three kids!' Gloria snapped. 'And my worthless husband would salivate like a dog in heat if he thought he had grounds to win a sizeable chunk of my money in a divorce settlement. I should have cut him loose as soon as I was elected to this office.'

'That wouldn't help me,' Tony complained. 'My wife worked to put me through law school . . . and I love my kids.'

'Quit sniveling like a child!' Gloria commanded. 'We've got to do something about this. I've got a re-election coming up. My challenger, that holier-than-thou, pasty-faced, prosecuting attorney, Paul Hanson, could use this to ruin me. He is already hammering the press about my being too lenient on crime and plea bargaining too many cases. If he gets hold of these . . . ' She didn't have to finish.

'Who could have taken them?' Tony wondered, taking a closer look. He clicked forward to see each of the five different pictures. 'These are all shots from above, and there's some kind of bars or something . . . like someone was watching from — '

'They were taken while we were in your office,' Gloria informed him angrily. 'That's your couch! This is the last time we were together!'

Tony groaned. 'And that room has a ceiling vent where the old air conditioning duct used to be, before the building was upgraded.'

Gloria cursed vehemently again, 'Yes! A perfect location for our peeping Tom!'

'Obviously,' Tony said. Then he suggested, 'Maybe we could dust for prints?'

'Don't be an idiot! We can't have the police involved.'

'What are we going to do?' Tony wanted to know. 'Both of our careers and marriages are on the line.'

Gloria controlled her voice. 'I think I know who is behind this. I checked the security log and there were only a few people in the building after hours that night. This guy is someone who would likely be up for blackmail, and he probably thinks we won't ever suspect him.'

'What do you want me to do?' Tony asked.

'You told me that Ernie was complaining about a troublesome parolee, one he was considering sending back to prison.'

'A real gem,' Tony said, thinking of the man his probation officer pal had mentioned. 'Chock Lincoln. The guy was picked up with a gun the other day and has a list of crimes two pages long. He was only released because of prison overcrowding.'

'Yes, I remember putting him away the last time. We dropped an assault charge and he pleaded guilty to robbery.'

'If he goes back inside he'll be there for eight more years,' Tony said.

'You think he might do us a favor to stay a free man?'

Tony's complexion blanched. 'Are you thinking of using him to try and get rid of this blackmailer?'

'He only has to scare him off and get back the pictures. Our blackmailer is a punk, and he's already fifty grand richer. If a real felon threatens him, he'll cower and run for cover like a scalded cat.'

'Yeah, but . . . ' Tony had to swallow his fear. He lowered his voice to a whisper, 'But what if it doesn't work?'

Gloria scowled at the man's weakness. 'Look, Tony, you and I both have a lot to lose

17

if these photos get out. I've already paid the blackmail demand, but I can't hide a second expense like that from my husband. He does the bookkeeping in our family and he would start asking questions. I placed some money in a private account before we were married, in case I needed some cash of my own. But paying for those pictures about cleaned me out. The only way we're going to be safe is to make sure no one else ever sees those pictures.'

'When you paid the money why didn't you get back the negatives?'

'What negatives?' she cried. 'They were from a cell phone. He promised to destroy the photos, but he could have saved them to a computer, or he might still have them in the phone's memory. There's only one way to make sure those pictures don't show up again. We have to frighten the creep into getting rid of the evidence and never opening his mouth.'

'Whatever you say, Glory, honey,' Tony assented passively. 'I'll get in touch with Ernie and have him put me in touch with Lincoln.'

'We can't tell anyone what this blackmail is about, Tony,' Gloria warned him. 'Neither of them can know any of the details.'

'No, I won't say anything about what we

have in mind,' Tony promised. 'Ernie owes me for keeping his brother out of jail a few months back on a Drunk Under the Influence charge. He'll cooperate. Then, if I offer to get the weapon charge dropped against Lincoln, the man ought to be willing to do whatever we want. Ernie won't be any the wiser about the details.'

Gloria picked up a piece of paper. She had already researched the information and had it ready. 'This is the target and his address. He rooms with another guy, so tell Lincoln we want no mistakes and no trail that can lead back to us.'

'What about the pictures?'

'Lincoln is to thoroughly scare the hell out of the blackmailer. Then he needs to collect any phones or computers and search the place for any stashed photos.'

'For something that involved, the man will probably expect payment.'

'We are keeping him out of jail!' Gloria declared. 'However . . . ' She took a moment to mull over the situation. 'Considering what we're asking, offer him a couple thousand dollars as an additional payment.'

'Do you have that much on hand?'

'It will leave nothing in my private account, but yes.'

'You know I'd help if I could.' Tony again

allowed the whiny tone to enter his voice, 'but, with three kids, and my wife no longer having a job — '

'Yes, yes,' Gloria cut him off, sick to death of hearing about his family. 'I know your situation.'

'I'll make a call and meet with Ernie this afternoon. With luck, he'll put me in touch with Lincoln in a day or two.'

'The sooner the better,' Gloria told him. 'We need a quick end to this blackmail scheme.'

★ ★ ★

Kari looked forward to Sundays and her weekly long-distance tryst with Jason. She had gradually turned the phone calls into an intimate and quixotic ritual. Shortly before the appointed time she would don an enticing outfit, apply her makeup and add a dab of expensive perfume. With romantic music playing softly in the background and two scented candles burning, she would lounge on the loveseat with her favorite pillow. A freshly poured Pepsi-over-ice would be in a glass, perched within reach on the coffee table. Once Jason was on the line she would stare at the framed photo that Reggie, Jason's

American cousin, had taken of Jason and her, the last time the three of them had been together. Over the next hour, she would talk to Jason of work, of dreams, of wishing they were together. And occasionally, during the conversation, she would close her eyes and try to envision his smoky-gray eyes, the half-smile on his face — often from humor or subtle teasing — and his neatly shorn tawny-brown hair. With his endearing voice and words of affection in her ears, she could almost feel his arms around her.

Most nights, after the call was over, she would get out a notepad and write him a letter. She usually sent off two or three each week, plus a number of emails, and he would do the same. Her mood was always a bit more gloomy on the days she didn't receive one of his letters or a lengthy email.

Presently the warmth of her thoughts from the previous night's telephone conversation was tucked away, replaced with a nervous apprehension. Before her was a naked interview, approaching a possibly hostile subject with no forewarning and no invite. It caused a roiling within her stomach and an icy chill to cling to her spine.

Kari pulled her car to the curb in front of the address for which she had been searching and stopped. It took a few moments, after switching off the engine, to collect her thoughts and her courage.

'Come on, chicken,' she taunted herself. 'This was your idea!'

Kari got out of the car, took out her pad and pencil and used the shoulder strap to secure her purse. Her heart pounded as she made her way up the narrow sidewalk, arrived at the house and rang the doorbell. This was above and beyond her job description, but the city was being overrun with drugs shipped in from another country. Someone had to do something.

The door opened and a young white man stood there, looking slightly down at her. He was in his early twenties, handsome in a feral, sinister sort of way: dark eyes, bushy brows, a face unshaven for at least two days, with shaggy black hair that was thick and needed a strong shampoo. He wore slippers, a white muscle-shirt and Levis.

'Whasup, sister?' He drawled the query.

Kari caught the whiff of liquor on his breath, but firmed her resolve.

'I'm looking for Juno Orozco. He lives here, doesn't he?'

He grinned salaciously. 'Yo, girl! If you want to party with Juno and me, you got to bring a friend. We been down since we was *shorties* in school — we share everything.'

'I'm from the *Sentinel*,' Kari said, ignoring his vulgar ogling and distasteful gangsta lingo. 'I only want to ask Juno a few questions. Is he here?'

'True-that, Miss Reporter,' he sneered. 'But Juno and me ain't lookin' to get our names lit up on some marquee.'

Kari didn't reply to that and he stepped back, holding the door open. She swallowed her terror and entered the apartment, to see that Juno was busy hooking up an Xbox to a big-screen television. He paused from examining an instruction book and looked at her.

'What do you want with me, lady?'

'I'm Kari Underwood, a reporter for the *Sentinel*.'

Juno laughed. 'A reporter?' Then throwing a curious glance at his friend. 'Dom, what kind of mischief you been up to?'

'Not my biznezz, brah,' Dom gave a droll reply. 'She come sliding up to the door askin' fo' you.'

Kari explained that she was trying to connect one of the local gangs to the marijuana fields back in the hills. Also, she had been told about a link to a major cartel in South America.

'Are you clowning with us?' Juno wanted to

23

know. 'You 'spect us to rat out one of the local gangs?'

'I was told you weren't actually a part of any gang,' Kari said. 'Your cousin is head of the Hard Corps, but you work at a garage.'

'What you talkin' about, foo?' Dom snickered. 'Juno and me would get balled up big time if we snitched to you.'

Juno agreed with a smirk of his own. 'A dude what runs his mouth don't have a long life on the streets, reporter lady.'

''Sides that,' Dom chimed in a second time. 'If we wanted to sing songs of woe and blow, I could fo' sho' serenade the DA herself.'

'DA Streisand?' Kari was incredulous and scribbled on her pad. 'How do you know her?'

Dom grinned. 'Hellfire, woman! Me and the lady is tight, though she's too busy hitting it on the side to worry herself 'bout little thangs like smack or some dog getting baked. You'd have better luck talking to that fizzle what shadows her.'

She frowned her incomprehension at his slang, but jotted most of it down. 'I won't use any names,' she tried again. 'And I'm willing to pay you for any information.'

'You expect to score poison pen from me on my own cousin?' Juno was impudent.

24

'Are you saying your cousin is involved with the cartel?'

'No, I ain't saying nuthin' about nuthin'!' Juno retorted. 'What I will say, is you're asking to get yourself strung up with your own pantyhose. What makes you think I ain't running with the Hard Corps?'

'Because Dom here works at the court-house. Plus, his father is Judge Westmoreland. The judge wouldn't allow his son to share an apartment with an active gang member, especially if he was tied to the drugs on the street.'

'Who told you about my dad?' Dom wanted to know, forgetting to use gangsta language.

'It's on record, being that you are an employee of the state government.'

'You is a ratchet fool, lady,' Juno spoke in a threatening tone. 'You don't write a word about us and we won't tell my cousin you were asking questions. Better for you — better for us!'

'But if it's a rival gang that's behind the — '

Dom took a menacing step toward her, ending her inquiry. He pressed up so close that Keri was forced to back up to keep their chests from touching. His eyes could have belonged to the devil himself, wicked and full of malevolence.

'You better roll, reporter lady,' he hissed the words — in plain American English this time. 'Or else you're going to have to pay for this visit . . . ' then said meaningfully, 'with something other than money.'

Kari fought down the urge to run from the house screaming at the top of her lungs. Instead, she controlled her panic and backed out on to the front porch. Attempting to salvage a sliver of pride, she said, 'If you should change your mind, any pertinent information would be worth a couple hundred dollars.'

'Shizzle my dizzle, lady!' Dom snickered, with a lecherous twist of his lips. 'Do we look like we are beggin' chips from some broad?'

Before she could respond he slammed the door in her face!

Kari was trembling from the encounter and it occurred to her that she might not be cut out for investigative field work. She wrote down the balance of what she could remember being said, including several words she didn't know. Her heart was still racing as she walked with weakened knees towards her car.

Although she had failed and been dismissed like an unwanted salesman, Kari's senses still functioned. She had the queer feeling that someone was watching her. Yet a glance over her shoulder told her it wasn't Dom or Juno.

Upon reaching her car she put away her notebook and purposely dropped her keys. As she squatted down to retrieve them she took a quick scan of the area. Even as her fingers took hold of the keys she noticed that a car was parked on the opposite side of the road, perhaps fifty yards down the street. A man was behind the wheel, but she couldn't make him out clearly. It wasn't a kid, nor an elderly person — perhaps in his thirties, dark complexioned, wearing a baseball cap and dark-glasses. The car was a blue Ford Taurus that had seen better days. It had a dented front fender and was in dire need of a wash job.

Kari climbed behind the wheel of her car and started the engine. As she pulled away from the curb she kept watch in her rearview mirror. The man did not follow her. To be certain, she turned quickly to the left, went a block, made a right turn and stopped. With her heart still beating hard and fast, she held her breath, waiting and watching.

Nothing.

After some moments, Kari released the air from her lungs and started her car moving again. With a last glance in the mirror to make sure no one was after her, she shook her head.

'That settles it, Kari Marie Underwood,' she said aloud. 'You are not cut out to be investigating drug cartels all by yourself!'

3

Things had been quiet around Sutton, so when DC Butterworth, one of two female detective constables on the force, received a call to check on a robbery, Jason offered to go along. Butterworth was used to a bit of superfluous attention from the male officers as she was quite attractive and had an amiable disposition. However, it was the first time Jason had made an offer to accompany her and she welcomed him along.

The burglary had taken place while the elderly widow was off playing bingo, a usual occurrence the same night each week. Several items of value were taken, but the greatest loss was a rare coin collection the woman's husband had gathered over the years. Once the victim had met them at the door DC Butterworth began listening to her tale and filling out a report, while Jason investigated the jimmied back door. There was no deadbolt or latch, only a keyed-entry single-cylinder knob with a turn button on the inside. It appeared someone had used a crowbar of some sort to break in.

'I just don't know what I'm going to do,' he

heard the aged lady sob. 'Henry said we could use them there coins for an emergency, if the need were ever great enough. I feel as if I betrayed his faith in me, you know?'

Butterworth consoled and questioned the woman as to who might have known about her bingo nights. Jason stopped listening when he spied a broken piece of plastic, lurking among some flowers planted next to the walk.

Holding the piece by the edges, he turned it over and discovered it was half of someone's bank card. It was perfectly clean, which meant it had not been lying there before yesterday's afternoon's shower. He glanced at the door and smiled.

The elderly woman was still lamenting her failure to protect something so valuable. DC Butterworth caught the serious look on Jason's face as he entered the room and stopped her from continuing.

'Do you happen to know someone with the last name of Kittle?' He posed the question to the victim.

'My sister's name is Kittle,' she answered. 'Her son, Mark, mows my lawn and sometimes runs errands for me.'

'Does Mark know about your bingo nights?'

The woman scowled. 'Yes, but Mark

wouldn't do something like this. Mark is a very pleasant sort.'

Butterworth recognized that Jason's questions were important. She left the woman's side and stepped over next to him.

'Did you find something?'

Jason held out the piece of broken plastic. 'I believe our thief tried to use this to picklock the back door. It probably got stuck and he broke it in half. Evidently, he didn't bother to pick up this piece, or he was in a hurry and didn't take the time to look for it.'

'Do you have an address for your nephew?' Butterworth asked the woman.

'Of course. It's in my directory next to the telephone.'

An hour later Mark Kittle had given up his loot and was booked for burgling his aunt's home. Jason let DC Butterworth deal with the report and take credit for the arrest. He saw her a bit later while he was having a sandwich in the lunchroom. She greeted him with a bright smile and hurried over to join him at the table.

'It was very good of you to let me be the officer of record concerning the nicking of Mark Kittle. I haven't had the chance to earn much recognition since I became a DC.'

'I'm confident you would have found the same bit of evidence once you'd finished talking to the victim.'

They ate their lunch quietly until Butterworth ventured another query. 'I've spoken to some of the others about you, gov.' She displayed a sheepish grin. 'Being that you are single and all.'

Jason was uncertain as to how to reply to that, so he waited for her to continue.

'I'm not in a relationship myself just now,' Butterworth murmured, a crimson flush beginning to color her cheeks. 'It's not that I don't have a number of offers, but I'm looking for something more than a good time. Know what I mean?'

Jason realized where this conversation was headed. He smiled politely. 'DC Butterworth — '

'Hermione,' she interrupted, giving him her first name.

Jason continued to smile. 'You are aware of the problems that arise with interdepartmental relationships?'

'I would be willing to risk it . . . with the right person,' she said pleasantly.

'I haven't told very many people, Hermione, but I am at the moment involved in a relationship.'

The smile faded at once. 'Oh! I didn't know.' She lowered her eyes, abashed at being so forward.

'It isn't something I wanted bantered around,' Jason went on, trying to ease Hermione's humiliation. 'The young lady actually lives in America.'

That prompted a curious look. 'America?' Then with a shake of her head. 'How on earth do you carry on a significant relationship with someone who's three thousand miles away across the blinking ocean?'

Jason laughed. 'It does pose certain intimacy problems.'

'But you're committed to her?'

'Yes. I believe she's worth the effort.'

The young lady's face brightened and her lips lifted in a slight smile. 'Then I'm happy for you, gov. I hope it works out.'

Relieved at her tactful response, Jason returned her smile and spoke sincerely, 'Thank you, Hermione. I hope you find someone special too.'

★　★　★

Juno Orozco took a drag on the rolled marijuana and glowered at Dom. They had been partying a few minutes before, but now their small rental house was empty except for the two of them.

'Man,' Juno complained, 'you got to quit roughing up your piece of tail. We could have had fun with them two slamming babes all friggin' night.'

'The silly biznatch got all hostile every time I tried to touch her,' Dom growled back. 'You'd think she had never given up her gold or something. I know that, when Lana was hangin' with your cousin he was always beatin' dem cakes.'

'Victor has the power, man,' Juno replied. 'You don't get to be *Caudillo* over the toughest gang around without you prove yourself. Victor's done it all, man.'

'Yeah, yeah, I've heard it all before,' Dom said sourly. 'Victor's the king.'

Juno passed the half-burned weed to Dom and picked up the bottle of tequila. 'All I'm saying is you got to back off of being so rough. There ain't many chicks who like getting knocked around till they're black and blue.'

'I hear you.' Dom snorted. 'I blew it tonight. I should have waited until she got her swerve on first. Once she was flying, she'd have come around easy.'

'You got it, man. Remember the four Fs: *find 'um, feel 'um* — '

'Awright,' Dom cut him off. 'Just skip to the *forget 'um* part and we're down.'

Juno paused from taking a drink and belched loudly. 'Hope Victor don't hear about that reporter snooping at our door. He's real touchy about anyone talking to the press.'

'Hey, man, we didn't tell her squat.'

'No, we didn't,' Juno agreed. 'But it's the idea, you know? Someone sees a reporter paying us a visit — next thing, we're getting our throats cut.'

'If you're worried 'bout it, call your cousin and give him the down low. He'll be cool with the way we handled her.'

'Yeah, maybe I'll do that later.'

'This having extra coin to spend is great.' Dom dropped his gangsta chatter and grew serious. He bobbed his head at the new television. 'Our two paychecks were barely covering the rent and eats. Taking that gal for a pile of money was a great idea.'

'You bet. We've got it made now — new TV, an Xbox 360 and all the games we want.' Juno displayed a smug expression. 'So long as we don't get too greedy, that cash cow is going to give us a healthy portion of milk for a long time.'

Dom grinned. 'Never knew so little work could pay so good.'

Juno started to laugh, then sat upright and gasped in alarm.

A bullet hit him in the middle of the chest, stifling his cry. He was driven back against the worn cushions of the old couch as a second round tore through Dom's throat. Both of them were drunk, stupefied from booze and the joint they had been smoking. Giving them no chance to escape or fight back, two more slugs ripped holes through each of their bodies. In a matter of seconds, both of their lives had ended.

★ ★ ★

Kari had accepted a dinner invite from her parents. As usual, they were concerned about her being so doggedly faithful to a man who lived across an ocean.

'Have you given any thought to that nice young man I introduced you to the other day?' her mother asked, after the meal was finished.

Kari was helping with clearing the table at the time. 'I imagine he will be a good catch for some girl.'

'Listen, daughter,' her father joined in, still in his kitchen chair but no longer sitting at the table. 'When you turn thirty you'll find that men are like parking spaces — all of the good ones are gone, and the rest are handicapped!'

'I believe I saw a bumper sticker to that effect,' Kari quipped. 'Are you no longer writing your own material?'

'We just don't like to see you pining over a man you will only see for a week or two each year!'

'You both wanted me to be in a relationship,' Kari reminded them. 'Well, this is the one I've chosen.'

'Yes, but to what end?' her mother wanted to know. 'Where does this relationship lead?'

'We haven't decided yet.'

'How do you know Jason isn't seeing other women?' her father inquired.

'I trust him completely.'

Her mother frowned. 'But he could be dating other girls, while you are sitting at home writing letters or waiting for his telephone call!'

'I'm happy with my life right now.' Kari dismissed their concern. 'I fully understand that Jason is a wonderful man and other women might try to take him from me. But I intend to follow my heart until Jason and I find a way to be together. If that doesn't happen, I'm willing to enjoy the closeness we share right now.'

'An incurable romantic,' her mother scoffed. 'Who would have ever thought that of you?'

Kari winked. 'I've seen the kind of love you and Dad have. It's what I want too.'

'Yes, but we weren't in different time zones

when we were courting,' her mother retorted.

'I saw your article in the paper.' Her father changed the subject. 'Drug crops being grown in the hills, a drug cartel supplying drugs to be sold on the streets and even in our schools. It's enough to make us want to move, except there's no place free of those vices any more.'

'It's getting worse all the time,' Kari said, anxious to turn the conversation away from her love life. 'One or more of the local gangs has an affiliation with the Colombian North Valley Drug Cartel, one of the biggest in all of Colombia. My editor won't let me name any names, because I can't get the proof I need.'

'I think you'd best stay away from that kind of reporting,' her father said. 'Those people working with the cartel play for keeps. You start poking at them with a stick and they'll do whatever it takes to shut you up.'

'You and my editor would get along nicely,' she remarked drily. 'He said the same thing.'

'Yes, well, even the government won't take on the gangs and drug lords. Every time they've tried it cost a fortune in money and lives and the results were nil. So long as people of all classes are hooked on drugs, and there's a ton of money to be made selling the stuff, there won't be enough law enforcement to stop the flow into this country.'

'It doesn't mean we should look the other way.'

'No, but it is best if you leave it alone,' her father warned. 'I'd rather see you move to England and marry the Brit than get involved in something that might get you killed.'

'Not to worry, Father. I drew a blank on my personal quest for information and Scott won't let me write anything critical enough to warrant a reprisal.'

'If you can stay for a while, we'll put on a movie and have some popcorn later,' her mother spoke up. 'We haven't watched *While You Were Sleeping* for a long time and we know it's one of your favorite movies.'

'Yes, it is, but I have some laundry to do at my apartment, and I have to finish an article on drunk drivers.'

'You know you're welcome anytime, daughter,' her father said.

She smiled. 'Yes, Daddy, I know.'

4

Kari took notes at the morning news briefing. The bodies found were known to have been involved with the Hard Corps gang. The speculation was that this had been an attack by a rival gang. The blanket statement didn't satisfy Kari. She waited until after most of the other reporters had left, then cornered Detective Louis Grady.

'I presume this is your case, Detective,' she said in greeting. 'I mean, you and Detective Hampton are the two premier investigators in the valley.'

Grady was genial, in his mid-thirties, carrying a few extra pounds; a happily married man who enjoyed his three kids. When it came to business, however, he was a professional and ignored her flattery.

'I don't have any additional information for you, Miss Underwood.'

'It might interest you to know I spoke to those two boys yesterday afternoon.'

He narrowed his gaze. 'And why would you be talking to them?'

'I was concerned about the rampant increase in drugs in the valley. I've got it from a credible source that one or more of the gangs is actually working with a Colombian cartel. It's rumored a major shipment comes in from Colombia every month.'

'And what did the two victims tell you about the drugs and the cartel?'

Kari sighed. 'Absolutely nothing.'

Grady accented the feebleness of her efforts with a snort of contempt.

'But it did appear that they had come into some money recently,' Kari pointed out. 'The big-screen television looked brand new and they were hooking up one of those expensive game players.'

'Do you enjoy living dangerously?'

'Not really,' Kari admitted, then asked, 'but it's true about the monthly shipment, isn't it?'

'No comment.'

'One of the two dead men is the son of Judge Westmoreland,' she challenged, looking for any shred of information. 'I'm sure the judge had something to say about this attack.'

'I'm not at liberty to quote anything the judge might have said during notification. If you sit tight and wait, I imagine he will comment on his loss publicly.' Grady's words were brusque, allowing his personal feelings to surface. He quickly masked his unease over the double murder. 'If this was the action of another gang, we'll find out who's responsible.'

'Come on, Detective,' Kari pleaded. 'I need something extra so my editor will let me stay on the case.'

Grady's lips curled upward in a smirk. 'I don't see a down side for me if Scott should assign someone else.'

'I was the one who helped you crack the Coin Killer case.' She referred to the serial murderer's nickname, awarded to him after the public learned of a quarter being placed in each of his victim's mouths. 'You owe me.'

'Your British boyfriend had a hand in helping you with that.'

'Anything you can give me would be greatly appreciated,' she continued her entreaty. 'Anything at all.'

Grady's stance weakened and he exhaled a breath in resignation. 'It appears someone entered the house and shot them both. The two vics were stoned on dope and tequila. It's clear neither of them was able to put up a fight.' He shrugged. 'No one saw anything, and the sound of gunfire in the Rose Park area isn't exactly unheard of. Most people who live on that street tend to duck for cover when a shot's fired, rather than run to the window and look to see what's happening. No witnesses have come forward as yet.'

'The judge's son was not a member of any

gang. Do you believe he was just in the wrong place at the wrong time?'

'No comment.'

'But Juno was a gang member . . . right?' she persisted. 'I mean, his cousin is the leader of the Hard Corps.'

'No comment.'

Kari showed her irritation by placing her hands on her hips and glaring at the detective. 'Is there anything at all you can tell me?'

'Your mascara is uneven,' he quipped.

'Thanks,' she said sourly. 'But you might want to be more accommodating.' He perked up like a hunting dog as she went on. 'It just so happens that I have some juicy information, and I'm tempted to make you wait until you have to read about it in print.'

'You said you got nothing when you interviewed Juno and Dom.'

'Nothing *from* them, but I might have something for you to look into.'

'All right,' Grady finally relented. 'The only odd thing about this attack is that the killer trashed the place. Don't know what he was looking for, but he took the victims' laptop computer and their cell phones.'

'That sounds like more than a simple hit.'

'It's all I've got for you, squirt.' He eyed her threateningly. 'Now give!'

Kari told him about seeing the car parked near the boys' house. She gave him a description of the vehicle and what little she could about the driver.

'That's it?'

'He didn't look like he was there by accident, and he definitely took notice of my arrival and departure. He could be the killer.'

'Or he could be a salesman, a drunk who was trying to sober up before driving, or someone having a meal in their car.'

'It's still something.'

'Yeah, yeah, it's something.' Grady jotted the information down in a notepad, then lifted a hand in farewell. 'Stay out of trouble, squirt.'

Kari flashed him a smile. 'It's not in my nature to get into trouble, Detective.'

There was no further exchange. Grady spun on his heel and walked over to join his less accommodating senior partner, Detective Hampton. The two of them departed the gathering and Kari was satisfied that she had gotten a little more information than everyone else.

* * *

Gloria stormed into the office that Tony shared with two other attorneys. Her flaming red hair was uncommonly frizzy and a lock dangled and bounced in front of one of her glaring green eyes. Seeing her stride smartly between the row of cubicles, Tony rose with unsteady knees to meet her.

'Mr. Martin!' Her voice was a trifle shrill, yet controlled enough so as to not draw undue attention. 'A matter has come up that needs your immediate attention. Please bring the notes about the case we discussed and come to my office.'

As she spun about on her three-inch heels, Tony grabbed a folder from his desktop and hurried after her. Her strides were such that he practically had to run to keep within a few feet of her.

They reached the hallway, but Gloria continued the rapid pace until she reached her outer office.

'No calls, Dotty,' she informed her secretary curtly. 'This shouldn't take but a few minutes.'

'Yes, ma'am,' the woman at the desk answered promptly.

Tony entered Gloria's office out of breath as she shut the door behind him. Then she marched in a circle, hands on her hips, her jaw tightly clenched. After a couple trips around the room to curb her ire, she stopped in front of the very subdued and quaking ADA.

'Tell me what on earth went wrong!' she hissed vehemently. 'How did Dom and Juno end up dead?'

Tony's head rotated back and forth as if on a swivel. 'I swear, Glory honey, I gave Chock Lincoln the very instructions we had agreed upon. He was supposed to scare Dom, grab his phone and computer and search for any pictures. That's it!'

'Well, it sure doesn't look as if he followed orders, does it?'

Tony groveled in angst and cowardice. 'He called me a few minutes ago and said he'd been seen, so he did what he had to do.'

Gloria cursed the killer, his parents and even his pets. When she had finished venting her wrath she glared at Tony. 'I didn't sign up for murder. This can't come back to us!'

'What can we do about it now?' Tony whimpered. 'Lincoln expects to be paid the two thousand dollars we promised.'

'Did he tell you how much money he found in the house?'

'A couple hundred dollars.'

'A couple hundred?' Gloria scowled. 'What about my fifty thousand dollars?'

'Lincoln claimed the only cash he found was on the victims.'

Gloria reined in her rage, summoning the training that allowed her to harness emotion and project control and rationality. It took several deeply drawn breaths, but she eventually eased her rigid stance.

'All right,' she said carefully. 'What's done can't be changed. We can only manage the fallout from Lincoln's asinine actions. We have to figure out what those two did with the rest of the money and get back those incriminating photos. Did Lincoln do that much of the job right?'

'He said he has their phones, an iPad, and the only computer in the house, but he didn't find any pictures during his search.'

'They must be on one of their phones or the hard drive on the computer. I'll go through everything, retrieve or destroy the pictures, and then you can discard the items where they won't be found.' She gazed at Tony with twin diamond-shard eyes. 'You go see Lincoln, pick up the stuff and pay him off. Tell the stupid goon to lay low for the time being. If anyone points a finger his direction, he'll have to leave the state.'

'I . . . I'm to meet with him this afternoon,' Tony stammered.

'You said Lincoln told you he'd been seen. By whom?'

'A female reporter from the *Sentinel* was at the house to talk to Juno and Dom. From his description it was Kari Underwood.'

Gloria felt her heart sink into her stomach. 'Not that little bloodhound! She'll cover this story like a coat of paint.'

Tony was immediately shaken. 'You think she got anything out of the interview with those two?'

'Who knows?' Gloria cried. 'We don't have any idea why she was there!' She smoothed her hair with her hands — fighting back the urge to yank it out by the handful. How had she gotten into this unholy mess?

Pondering her options, she said, 'It would behove Lincoln to give us a hand with that female snoop.'

'Why should he do that?' Tony wondered.

'We need the police to keep looking at Juno and his link to drugs and gangs.'

'So you think Underwood was there to interview Juno?' Tony said, then concluded, 'Because his cousin is the leader of the Hard Corps.'

'It makes sense. Everyone knows Juno isn't a member of the gang, but the reporter must have thought he could tell her something.' As a thought popped into her head, she snapped her fingers.

'Yes!' she exclaimed. 'I know what this is about. Underwood wrote a piece about drugs coming into the valley. She even mentioned the possibility of a connection with a cartel somewhere in South America.'

'How does that help us?'

'It's the angle needed to make this whole thing go away,' Gloria explained patiently. 'No one messes with those international drug consortiums.'

'So what do you want to do about Underwood?'

Gloria replied, 'Chock Lincoln put us in this bind by killing those two boys. It's up to him to sell the idea that this is gang related. He needs to give the reporter a scare!' She repeated. '*Scare* — not kill!' Next she added, 'And he needs to search her place the first chance he gets.'

'You really think she has some information at her apartment?'

'Probably not, but it will keep the cops busy. If they think Underwood knows something about drugs, they will be chasing after her and looking the wrong way. Once the cops decide this is gang-related, they will stop seeking anything tied to anyone or anything else . . . namely blackmail and us.'

Tony didn't wag his tail and pant, but he was as eager to please as a lonely pet. 'OK, Glory honey. You're smarter than the cops and that reporter combined. This will work.'

Gloria reached out and tapped him on the chest with a long, manicured fingernail. 'Tell

Lincoln no mistakes,' she warned. 'I mean it.'

He didn't try to make his voice work. Instead, he bobbed his head and hurriedly scampered out of the room.

Gloria realized her teeth were clenched so hard they began to ache. She felt a great fear in her chest, a dark pit of regret and contrition. A simple case of adultery had turned into a recipe for murder. Resisting a divorce, so that she could avoid a scandal and hang on to her material wealth might now cost her everything she owned . . . even her freedom.

Don, she cursed her husband, *why couldn't you have been the man I thought I married!*

* * *

Back at the news agency, Kari was typing away when Marge Taylor, her immediate supervisor, joined her at her desk. Kari told her about the search of the dead pair's home and the missing items. It was the extra bit of information she had wormed out of Detective Grady. The woman gave a nod of approval and changed the subject.

'Have you spoken to Jason lately?'

'We email one another daily, write letters back and forth, and we talk on the phone every Sunday. It's a difficult courtship, being so far apart.'

Marge grinned at her statement. 'What era did you say you were born in? *Courtship?*'

'I'm a little old-fashioned for the times.'

'Well, I have to admit, your man impressed me,' Marge commented. 'He helped to clear up my brother-in-law's death in about ten minutes flat.'

Kari experienced a warm flush at the term *your man*, but hid it quickly. 'Yes,' she replied. 'It's fortunate he was familiar with the use of those cardboard compactors from a job he worked at while attending college. He knew there was a trick to bypassing the safety switch so the compactor would engage without the door being closed.'

Marge gravely shook her head. 'My sister claimed her husband didn't let anyone know he had been seeing a doctor. With his black hair, dark complexion, and working with a good many Latino employees, he spoke Spanish well enough to pretend to be an undocumented worker from Mexico. He gave a false name to the Medicaid people when he went to the clinic. After he was diagnosed with pancreatic cancer, he knew he only had a few months to live. He had hoped my sister would collect on his accident insurance, which would have been ten times as much as the normal death policy.'

'One has to admire his courage. Being crushed to death does not sound like a fun way to die.'

'Neither does dying from cancer of the pancreas.'

Kari agreed and Marge wandered off to check on the other people she supervised. Getting back to her story, Kari tried to find the words to hold the reader's attention. The motive for the murder was unknown. The briefing had mentioned that a couple of girls were at the apartment shortly before the shooting. That might be important. Perhaps the motive was jealousy from an angry ex-boyfriend, or one of the girls might have been from a rival gang, prompting a deadly reprisal. And, in spite of no one believing that Juno and Dom dealt in drugs, they might have tried their hand at it and ended up dead for the effort.

But why take their phones and computer? Was there important information on one of those devices? It seemed the only reason for the theft. Lastly, there was the unobtrusive man who watched from his car. Could Kari really have seen the killer?

'Hey, girlfriend!' Dee arrived with a smile. 'It's time to give your brain a rest. Let's go to the break room and you can tell me about dinner with your folks last night. I'll bet you had a wild old time.'

'Let me finish this,' Kari said. 'It's about ready to send to Scott's desk.'

Dee looked over her shoulder. 'Oh, yeah, the gang shooting. I'm not one to pass judgment, but a couple of bangers getting their due won't make me lose any sleep.'

'Hum, that sounds like *judgment* to me.'

Dee waved a hand to dismiss Kari's sarcasm. 'I mean it! They peddle drugs at the schools, they own the streets, they destroy landmarks, walls and fences with their disgusting graffiti. Who's going to miss a couple of bangers?'

'I tried to interview them both earlier the very day they were killed. They ran me off like a stray dog. Juno seemed pretty harmless and Dominick . . . well, he's Judge Westmoreland's son.'

Dee sucked in her breath. 'Westmoreland?' She sobered at the news. 'Wow, that's not good. He's next in line for the State Supreme Court. This is going to hit the fan like you know what!'

Kari gave a last look at the article and punched the send button, forwarding it to Scott's computer. 'Done,' she announced, eager to put the murders from her mind. 'Let's go see if there are any donuts left.'

5

The Honorable Judge Garth Westmoreland sat on the leather-bound couch in his living room. His daughter, Constance, was seated on one side of him and his eldest son, Benjamin, on the other. Constance worked for a marketing company and Benjamin owned a small construction company. All three of them appeared red-eyed and weary.

'We know this is hard on all of you,' Grady said, beginning the interview. 'We'll keep this short and leave you to grieve and take care of burial arrangements and the like.'

'Ask your questions,' the judge said somberly.

'We believe Juno Orozco was the likely target for this attack.' Hampton was the one to put forth their summation. 'With his cousin running the Hard Corps gang, someone could have been sending a message to Victor.'

'As for your son,' Grady interjected. 'I noticed he didn't have any gang tats.'

'No,' Benjamin was the one to reply. 'Dominick liked to spout trash talk, trying to sound like some rapper, but he never joined a gang. Him and Juno became best friends way back in elementary school. It was partly because they were so close that Dad and Mom never insisted that Dom attend a private school. In the past couple years, they both got jobs and were sharing a rented house together.'

Judge Westmoreland clarified the situation. 'When Victor took over as leader of the Hard Corps, I tried to break up Dom and Juno's friendship. I was afraid Victor would force them both to become active members. But by that time Dom was too old to order about. Then, after my wife died, Dom pretty much ignored me altogether.'

'Dominick was the youngest of our family,' Constance said, making her presence felt for the first time. 'He was bound to be a little spoiled.'

'Yes,' agreed Benjamin. 'His good looks and great smile could get him anything he wanted when Mom was alive. She died of a cerebral hemorrhage when Dom was sixteen. By that time Connie and I had already moved out and were on our own.'

'And I was working long hours in court these past few years. I didn't see much of Dom, even when he was living at home.' Garth displayed guilt. 'I didn't have enough time for my boy. I let him do whatever he wanted after Phyllis died.'

'I seem to remember he got into trouble a time or two, didn't he?' Hampton asked the question, but he and Grady knew the answer.

'Dom was popular with the girls,' Connie volunteered. 'But he always had a temper too. If the girl didn't behave exactly the way he wanted, Dom would often drop them flat.'

'Or even get a little physical with them,' Hampton expanded on that subject. 'Two different complaints were filed concerning his being abusive.'

The judge waved his hand to dismiss the allegations. 'He was high-strung and selfish, but he wasn't a bad boy. He missed his mother and sometimes expected more from a woman than she wanted to give. I tried to get him some professional help, but . . . ' He heaved a sigh. 'Anyway, the charges were dropped both times. No one was severely injured and I believe Dom had begun to treat women with more respect.'

'The reason I bring it up, Judge,' Hampton continued, 'is that witnesses said there were a couple of girls visiting the two victims shortly before the shooting. We have to consider the possibility that there was some kind of fight or disagreement between them. Perhaps one of the girls complained to a friend or relative about Dom. That might have been what prompted the shooting.'

Benjamin countered at once. 'Dom's temper was a problem, but it seldom got out of hand when he was with Juno. Juno knew how to control him.'

Constance agreed. 'Yes, the only complaints against Dom were when he was alone with a girl.'

'Getting back to Juno,' Grady said, 'he had the gang tattoo on his arm. Was he a full-fledged member of the Hard Corps?'

'Yes and no,' Benjamin answered. 'He was a member, but he didn't really hang around his cousin much. Juno belonged because it was expected of him. Dom said Juno hardly ever went over to Victor's place or did any running around with the gang. Juno worked at a Jiffy Lube, changing oil and filters on cars. He was always a pretty good kid.'

Hampton bobbed his head. 'I did a background check on him, and he didn't have any arrests. I also spoke to the gang unit and they said the same thing — Juno pretty much stayed out of trouble.'

'Regardless, with him being Victor's cousin, we have to consider that this murder could be intended to send a message to the Hard Corps,' Grady surmised, 'That said, we still need to ask if there is anything else you can tell us? Do you know if either of them were having personal problems with anyone? Were there any threatening messages left on their phones, slashed tires on one of their cars . . . anything like that?'

Garth exchanged looks with his kids and shook his head. 'Nothing that we knew about.'

'We have to consider that the boys might have known something or had some special information,' Grady continued. 'It appears they spent a lot of money in the last few weeks and their place was tossed. The assailant took their phones and computer. It's obvious they were getting money from some place and also that the killer was looking for something special.'

'I can't imagine what it could be,' the judge said.

'How about a girlfriend?' Hampton wanted to know. 'Do you have any idea who the girls were at their apartment?'

'We've no clue.' Benjamin was the one to respond. 'But then, I hadn't seen Dom in a couple of weeks. Last time we spoke, he was using street trash talk, you know, gangsta slang. I hardly understood a thing he said.'

Constance added, 'Dom was terrible about keeping in touch.'

'I only saw him for a few minutes at a time, usually when I ran into him at the state building. He was working as a janitor,' the judge informed them. 'Dom would occasionally drop by for a meal, but that's about all. If he had a special girl, he never spoke of it or brought her over to meet me.'

'Thanks for your time, Your Honor,' Grady said. 'We thank you two as well,' he added, speaking to Constance and Benjamin. 'We're very sorry for your loss, and we'll do everything we can to find out who killed Dominick.'

'Get to the bottom of this,' Judge Westmoreland said tightly. 'If this turns out to be over drugs, the DA and I will bring the combined weight of our offices down on those dealers. We've been looking the other way for far too long. We've let the gangs run free, without a lot of interference, so long as they didn't involve innocent bystanders. But if it turns out drugs and gangs are responsible for my son's death, I will use my position and influence to make every one of those delinquents pay.'

Constance patted her father's arm. 'Dad, these gangs often resort to terror and killing, You can't put a stop to it all by yourself.'

'This was not the act of one gang-banger or drug-dealer shooting another one!' he declared. 'This killing involved an innocent boy — my boy! This was one murder too many. I want the perpetrators found . . . and punished!'

★ ★ ★

Kari made a dozen calls to contacts and sources, then touched base with the cop in the gang unit. She dared only text Rick Cory, as it was not wise to call him directly. He had a street source nicknamed Radar — like the character on the old *MASH* TV series — except the Confidential Informant was not psychic, he was connected. He knew much of what went on and who was responsible for it. He was one of the few guys who managed to be on good terms with most every gang in the valley. According to Rick, Radar often passed along good information but nothing that could be traced back to him. Evidently Radar was keen on prolonging his own life. As for Rick, he had assumed control of the gang unit and the drug related shootings had dropped by nearly fifty per cent. However, communicating with the media could mean an end to his career, so he had to be careful whom he talked to and about what. He did respond a short while later but he had no information. He confirmed that Juno was not an active member of the gang, so it was unlikely he would have had any solid information concerning drug shipments or the like.

She thanked him for his help and decided to go visit Juno's sister. She might be able to shed some light on who was behind the attack.

Kari went to the parking garage, got into her car and drove along the winding path from the upper level until she reached the street exit. She engaged the brake and paused, squinting from the bright glare of the sun, to look for an opening in the heavy downtown traffic. There was a sudden *pop!*

A sprinkle of glass stung Kari's right arm and cheek. She gasped in shock when a second *pop!* shattered another small hole in the passenger side of the windshield! She instinctively ducked and sank down into the bucket seat.

Panic prompted her to react. She shifted into reverse and stepped on the gas. The car lurched rearward into the parking garage until she was well back from the street. Kari rose up quickly to see where she was going and slammed on the brakes.

Fortunately, no one had been behind her and she missed the nearest concrete girder by mere inches. Sitting there, foot still on the brake, her pulse thundering wildly against her temples, she began to shake. It was the most severe trembling she'd ever experienced. It was all she could do to draw air into her lungs. Her knuckles turned white from gripping the steering wheel, but she couldn't seem to let go.

Someone honked and an involuntary scream was ripped from her throat.

Moments later a face appeared outside her window. It was Lyle Tanner, a middle-aged man who worked in printing.

'Kari! What's the matter?' He had to shout due to the window being up. 'Are you all right?'

Regaining enough composure to raise one hand from the steering wheel, she recouped the strength to lower the window.

'L-Lyle,' she stammered. 'Someone . . . ' she gasped for a breath. 'Someone shot at me!'

He immediately took notice of the holes in the glass. 'Good Lord!' he cried. 'Are you hit? Are you all right?'

Kari noticed two small blood specks on her exposed arm, likely from the shattered glass. Then she touched her cheek, found another spot of blood and felt a tiny broken shard.

'No . . . and yes . . . I think so.' She still had no air in her lungs. 'I . . . ' Unable to say more, she reached down and shut off the car engine. With a small measure of rationality returning, she also thought to put the car in 'park', so it wouldn't roll.

'You're white as a bed sheet, Kari,' he told her gently. 'Take several deep breaths and let each one out slowly. I'll call the police.'

Kari tried desperately to inhale, but her body seemed unwilling to cooperate. Lyle made an emergency call and then opened the car door. She could see his mouth moving, but didn't hear his words right away. Then as he continued to try and calm her, she finally let out a breath, and was coherent.

'I didn't see anything,' she said. 'It happened so fast.'

'Sit tight,' he said. 'The police are on their way.'

★ ★ ★

The captain approached Grady's desk and stopped, displaying a look of impatience.

'Uh, we've come up with nothing concrete, Capt'n,' Grady said weakly. 'Victor has agreed to talk to us, so we'll see if he can give us anything. According to the guys in the gang unit, there isn't any word on the streets about the Hard Corps being at war with any of the other gangs.'

'No more than usual,' Hampton added. 'We know there is at least one of the gangs tied up with the Colombians. Could be there is some concern Juno knew about a shipment or something.'

'This is about the murder of Judge Westmoreland's son!' the captain reminded them hotly. 'We need answers!'

Grady said, 'Our favorite reporter visited them a few hours before they were shot. Then we know a couple of girls stopped by for a short time. We've got men scouring the neighborhood to try and learn the identity of those two girls. We think one was an ex-girlfriend of Victor's. We're hoping they might provide us with some kind of motive. Plus, every snitch on the street is looking to score information about this. The word is out that we're paying top dollar for any leads.'

'I noticed that Miss Underwood not only dropped by their house, she's the one who wrote the story in the paper.'

'We drew the short straw there,' Hampton complained. 'She'll be hounding us about anything and everything we learn.'

'I don't want her getting a free hand on this,' the captain said. 'We don't need a nosy reporter in the middle of our investigation.'

'You're right,' Grady said. 'And she proved what a blood-hound she can be. If she gets the scent, she'll follow it to the ends of the earth.'

'And drag us along with her,' Hampton lamented.

'I feel a need for my stomach medicine,' the captain complained. 'Every time I think I have my ulcer under control . . . ' He didn't have to finish.

'We'll let you know when anything new develops on the Westmoreland case,' Grady volunteered.

The captain left them. When he was out of earshot, Hampton leaned over closer to Grady. 'There's one positive thing we have on our side. Without the Brit being involved, we only have to ride herd on Underwood.'

'You're right, Ham. Maybe our favorite lady reporter will be content to simply report the news, rather than trying to create it.'

'You're just trying to make me happy.'

'Speaking of happy, I've got a lot of unhappy people for us to check out on this double murder.' Grady returned to their current case. 'Any one of the other gangs may have had reason to strike at the Hard Corps.'

'I'm not sure talking to Victor is going help. He'll be more interested in payback than helping us.'

'We're going to need a break to stop a gang war, Ham.'

'So how many names have you got on our list to interview?' Hampton asked. 'I mean besides Victor Orozco?'

Grady took his gun from the top drawer of his desk and slipped it on to his belt. He joined Hampton and headed for the door before answering.

'We'll start with about twenty. But that's before we include outside gang members from all over the city.'

'That's just great,' Hampton's voice was thick with cynicism. 'This would be tough enough if it was only Victor's brother. With a judge and the district attorney breathing down our necks, we'd better not miss anything.'

The phone rang for Hampton. It was Peggy from Dispatch but there was no time to make any small talk. She blurted the news and he grabbed hold of Grady's arm.

'Thanks!' was his response before he slammed down the receiver.

'What's up?' Grady asked, surprised at the shocked look on his partner's face.

'Someone just took a shot at Kari Underwood!'

6

By the time the detectives arrived Kari had control of her shaking and had some color back in her complexion. She was sitting behind her steering wheel, with the car door open. She had been treated by a paramedic for the minor cuts and removal of a couple tiny shards of glass. She had just completed an incident report with a uniformed cop when an unmarked car pulled up out in the middle of the street. Two familiar men got out. One went to speak to a uniform while the second hurried into the parking garage and up to where she was sitting.

'What the hell are you into, Miss Underwood?' Grady demanded to know, puffing from the exertion of running up the driveway's incline. 'Who shot at you?'

'I didn't see anyone,' she replied. 'I pulled out to the street far enough to check for an opening in the traffic, and the window exploded.'

'We talked to a couple witnesses who heard two shots,' the policeman who had taken the report informed Grady. 'They thought it sounded like a large-caliber rifle and came from across the road, somewhere up high. However, we haven't found anyone who saw the shooter.'

'I want all the nearby traffic cams looked at, plus any other security cameras that might show us the buildings across the street. Get people to check the rooftops and see if anyone saw a person who could have been carrying a gun. I want every office and room in that building checked; talk to anyone and everyone coming from, going to, or residing in the building.'

'We've started a canvas and called in additional units,' the cop replied.

'Good work.' Grady dismissed the man. Then he reached into the car, placed a consoling hand on Kari's shoulder and looked directly into her eyes.

'Are you sure you're not hurt?'

'No. I got sprinkled with a few tiny pieces of glass. It didn't even require any bandaging.'

'Thank goodness for that.'

Kari motioned to the adjacent seat cushion. 'I think one of the bullets went into the passenger seat. I heard it hit.'

'We've got forensics on the way. They'll remove the bullet and look for the second one too. You did hear two shots?'

'I didn't actually hear the shots, but I can

count the holes in the glass.' She was still dazed by the attack. 'Why would anyone shoot at me?'

Grady scowled at her. 'You've been sticking your nose where it doesn't belong. You did a piece on the drug cartel and talked to Juno Orozco. Considering Juno got himself killed shortly after your visit, someone must think you know something.'

'All Juno told me was to get lost.'

'Our shooter must think he told you something worthwhile,' Grady said. 'You admitted to knowing about a drug shipment coming in from Colombia each month. You might have asked the wrong question when you were snooping around.'

Kari swallowed hard, fearful that this might only be the beginning of her woes. 'But I didn't learn anything about drugs coming into the valley,' she murmured weakly. 'I really didn't.'

'You might want to work that information into your article when you write about being shot at,' Grady advised. 'We can hope whoever is responsible for this shooting will read the story and believe you.'

Kari perused the punctured windshield. 'Any idea if comprehensive insurance pays for bullet damage?'

Grady grunted his doubt. 'I'll check back

with you later. Ham and I have an interview with Juno's brother. We need to go talk to him.' He hesitated, then added: 'And I'll make sure he knows you didn't learn anything from Juno about any drug shipments.'

'Thank you, Detective Grady,' Kari said sincerely. 'I appreciate your help . . . and your concern.'

He sighed. 'Try not to get into any more trouble.'

★　★　★

Victor Orozco had tats on both arms, his neck and the knuckles of both hands. Four diamond-studded earrings decorated his earlobes and his black hair hung to his shoulders. With a face like an angry gargoyle, he bared his teeth in a sneer whenever he replied to either Hampton or Grady.

'Someone took a shot at a reporter a few minutes ago.' Grady tried to rattle the man's cage. 'If we find out you were behind that, you'll never see the light of day again!'

'Hey, man, most of my guys don't read the paper. You ain't gonna do no good trying to jack me around for something like that.'

'Maybe it's one of your rivals,' Hampton

70

tried again. 'You having trouble with one of the other gangs?'

'Nobody messes with the Hard Corps,' he drawled. 'We own the streets.'

'How about the 39th Street Lobos?' Hampton queried. 'They don't let anyone tread on their turf.'

'That's over on the east side, *Mr. Policeman.*' He slurred the title, as if it left a bad taste in his mouth. 'We don't worry about that side of the hill. Let the Lobos brag about their little piece of the valley; they know better than to cross our boundaries.'

'Someone took out your cousin.'

Victor's expression darkened at once and he regarded them with eyes full of hate. 'We'll find out who did it, Mr. Policeman. You don't have to worry about it none.'

'We don't want a war in the streets, Victor,' Hampton warned. 'If you bangers kill each other, that's fine with us. But this time an innocent man was killed.'

Victor laughed derisively. 'You couldn't be talkin' about Dominick. That homie had a rep for breaking hearts . . . and about every other bone in a girl's body.'

'We know he abused a girl or two,' Grady said.

The sneer again. 'You need to catch up with news of the socially élite, Detective.

Dominick never wanted what was offered freely. He was a perv who enjoyed the fight and submission.'

'You're saying he preferred to beat up girls,' Hampton deduced.

'The boy liked it rough. That's all I'm saying.'

'And Juno? Why would anyone go after your cousin?'

Victor's expression grew cold. 'That's something I'm gonna find out.'

'I told you, we don't want a war on our hands,' Hampton warned him again.

'Won't be no war,' Victor replied easily. 'Maybe a massacre, but no war.' With another smirk, 'And if you don't like the smell of burning pork, you and your boys in blue will stay out of our way.'

'I could arrest you for threatening a police officer,' Hampton advised him.

The gang leader displayed a completely innocent mien. 'I swear, Your Honor,' he pretended to plead his case, 'it was grief over the loss of my cousin that caused me to call them detective pigs uncomplimentary names without thinking. I'm a law-abiding citizen, a pillar of the community. Ask anyone.'

'Get out of my sight,' Hampton snorted. 'We're done.'

Victor rose to his feet and ran a hand

through his unkempt and greasy-looking hair. 'It's about time,' he said. 'I could get a bad name, hanging around this here sty with you porkers.'

'Keep working your mouth and you'll be hanging by your thumbs!' Hampton jeered.

Victor grinned at the impotent threat and left the interview room.

'Glad you didn't let him get under your skin,' Grady teased, once the gang leader was out of earshot. 'I'm always telling Kitten' (his pet name for his wife) 'how mild-mannered you are.'

Hampton's unhappy expression relayed his dissatisfaction concerning the interview.

'Let's head for home,' Grady said, glancing at the timepiece on his wrist. 'We'll start again tomorrow.'

★ ★ ★

Jason was sitting in the cafeteria when the desk sergeant, Nebo Riley, hurried over to speak to him. 'Call from the States for you,' Riley reported, an anxious look on his face. 'I tried to transfer it to your phone but it wouldn't go through.'

Jason removed his mobile. 'This sod-awful contraption! I've put in a new battery twice and made three requests for a new phone. It hasn't worked right since I went to the States last year.'

'I put the call on my own mobile,' Riley informed him, holding it out for him to use.

'Thanks, Riley. You're the best desk sergeant we ever had.'

Riley didn't reply, allowing Jason to push the 'mute' button so he could use the phone.

'Jason Keane here,' he said.

'Jason! It's Reggie. Reggie Cline, your cousin.'

'Of course, Reggie,' Jason said warmly. 'It's good to hear your voice again. What's happened? Why are you calling me?'

'Kari didn't want me to tell you this, but I thought you ought to know.'

When he didn't continue, Jason prompted him. 'OK, so what is it she won't tell me, but I ought to know?'

'Someone shot at her yesterday. I've been awake all night but — '

'Shot at her!' Jason exclaimed. 'Who shot at her?'

Reggie began again. 'Well, I waited until morning to call you — it's a little after six, so I thought — '

'Tell me what happened, Reggie.' Jason cut off his meandering chatter.

Reggie explained about the shooting and said the police had no suspects. He added that there might be a connection with a double murder, but there was no way of knowing if that were true.

'You're sure she's all right?'

'Yeah, Jason, I talked to her last night. That's how I knew she wasn't going to tell you about it. She claimed it was probably a random thing or maybe a mistake. The police were going to talk to a couple gang leaders and try and clear it up. She wrote a piece for the paper a few days ago concerning drugs in the valley. She doesn't think it had anything to do with the attack, but she doesn't really know.'

'The police and gang leaders? Concerning Kari and this attack?' Jason mulled over the information aloud. 'Why would a gang be after her?'

'The article she wrote mentioned the Colombia drug cartels being mixed up with one or more of the local gangs. It could have been the motive for the shooting.'

'I'll be there as soon as I can.'

'Whoa there, cuz!' Reggie exclaimed. 'Kari will scald my hide if you come rushing over here because I told you about this. It's why she warned me not to say anything.'

'You better keep your distance from her until I arrive then, because I'm going to speak to my DSI straight away. I'll let Kari and you both know when to expect me.'

'I guess I can't stop you, so I'll be happy to see you again,' Reggie said. 'I'll have your room ready. Just need to put on fresh sheets.'

'I'm grateful for the hospitality, Reggie. I'll see you soon.'

★   ★   ★

Kari had never met Gloria Streisand but knew her from press interviews. She was a natural redhead, with beautiful, below-the-shoulder-length hair. Her green eyes were a rich emerald and her complexion was as smooth and fine as porcelain. A youthful thirty-five, she was shapely enough to be considered voluptuous.

Gloria was also an excellent speaker, with a strong voice and carefully measured conviction. It offset any notion that she was overly feminine or too soft for her job. Her record for prosecuting was sound and she seldom lost a major case.

She was businesslike, sitting next to Grady with perfect posture, attired in a neatly tailored suit. The three of them were alone in the interview room.

'I read your column about drugs in our parks,' said Gloria, opening the conversation. 'You mentioned there might be a connection between one of the local gangs and a drug cartel in Colombia.'

'Yes, but I didn't name names.' Kari shrugged, 'I was never able to find out which gang or gangs might be involved.'

'The police think that might be why you were shot at.'

'It's one theory,' Grady corrected. 'I told the DA that you also talked to the two boys who were killed: Dominick Westmoreland and Juno Orozco. We have to consider that the shooting might be related to that visit.'

'I don't see how. Those two didn't give me any information.' Kari made a helpless gesture. 'I was trying to get a lead on which gang might be connected to the Colombians, but Juno was not forthcoming. As for Dominick, he was busy ogling me and making crude remarks to try and impress me as to what a big man he was.'

'Did you speak to them about anything outside of the gang issue?' Gloria wanted to know. 'Maybe you touched on another subject that was more sensitive than you realized.'

Kari wondered at the odd glint of interest in the woman's eyes. 'No, they were both very tight-lipped and gave me nothing of value.'

Gloria continued the stare, a trait that probably intimidated many guilty subjects.

'You're sure? Nothing that might have implied that they were involved in something illegal to make a lot of money?'

'They did have some brand-new toys — a wide-screen television, and Juno was connecting a game of some kind. He had just taken it out of the box and there was a stack of unopened DVDs on the coffee table. When I offered to pay them for information they pretty much laughed at me.'

The DA shifted her gaze to Grady. 'If that's the truth — if she got no information — why would someone target her?'

The detective displayed an equal puzzlement. 'It has to be related to the gangs or drugs. I scanned her articles for the last month and Miss Underwood hasn't covered anything else of major importance.'

Gloria pondered on his answer. 'The logical assumption is that someone from a gang linked to the cartel believes she discovered something about the importing or distribution of drugs.'

'It does seem a likely motive for the shooting,' Grady agreed.

'Any leads from the bullets that forensics recovered?'

'They are a .308 caliber, a popular gun with deer hunters. We've compiled a list of nearly a hundred registered owners. There's probably twice that many unregistered.'

Gloria scrutinized Kari for a long moment. 'And there's no other reason for anyone to be shooting at you? No jealous boyfriend? No fights or feuds with anyone? No clandestine investigation you are running on your own?'

'No, ma'am. Far as I know, I don't have an enemy in the world.'

'It might not be related,' Grady interjected, 'but Miss Underwood saw a car parked up the street from the boy's home. She didn't get a good enough look at the guy behind the wheel to give us a description, but there's a chance it was the killer. He might have thought she could identify him.'

'Have you any leads on the man?'

'No, but he was driving a Ford Taurus with a banged-up front fender.'

Gloria rose to her feet. 'All right. We're done here, Detective. Please keep my office informed of any pertinent information.'

'We'll let you know as soon as we find something, Ms District Attorney.'

The woman left and Grady let out a breath that he seemed to have been holding. 'Whew!' He sighed his relief. 'That woman reminds me of my fourth-grade principal. She could take one look at you and know if you had done anything wrong. I remember ducking into a bathroom to avoid meeting her in the hallway one day.' He displayed a silly grin. 'Turns out I stepped into the girls' lavatory! And that is exactly where she was headed!'

Kari laughed. 'How did you explain what you were doing in there?'

'I didn't!' he replied. 'I hid in the first stall until the bell rang and everyone was back in class.'

'If she'd caught you . . . ?'

Grady held up a hand to stop her and said, 'I wouldn't have lived long enough to have become a cop.'

7

Flying economy from London on the overnight flight was not much fun. As he had purchased his ticket only one day in advance, Jason was stuck in the middle seat of the middle aisle. And one situation he had never been comfortable with was trying to sleep while sitting up straight . . . especially with a person on either side trying to use his shoulder as a pillow!

With the wearisome overseas flight behind him, he purchased a Chicago morning paper at the terminal gate area of the O'Hare airport. As he still had a while to wait before his connecting flight to Salt Lake City, he bought a cup of tea from a coffee-and-bagel shop. He found his gate and took a seat on the outer fringe of the boarding area. After a sip or two of the hot liquid, he decided it wasn't the worst tea he had ever tasted — only the worst since he had last been in the States.

An article about two bullets being fired through the windshield of a reporter's car was so small he almost missed it. He saw it was written by Kari Underwood and mentioned the probability that it was a case of mistaken identity! However, it did touch on a double murder and an interview the reporter had been involved with sometime earlier. One of the victims had been the cousin of a gang leader for a group called the Hard Corps. The other had been the son of a highly respected judge. There were no suspects, but a shooting like that often provoked a deadly response. The unwarranted attack might have been a warning for newspeople to steer clear of gang business.

Jason reread the article and heaved a sigh. 'Kari, love, I hope you haven't gotten yourself involved in another deadly case!'

★　★　★

Gloria Streisand entered the judge's chambers. He stood at the picture window, staring out at the nearby buildings, his hands locked thoughtfully at the small of his back.

'Judge Westmoreland,' Gloria said softly. 'I would have contacted you at your house, but I wanted to personally and privately offer my condolences for your loss.' The judge's head ducked slightly as he suffered his loss in silence. When he did not reply, she continued. 'I want you to know our office is making this our number one priority. Every detective,

82

every officer on the street and every member of the gang unit is working on this. We'll find whoever killed your son.'

'Anything on that shooting at the parking garage yesterday?'

Gloria explained about her interview with the reporter and Grady. 'About all we have at this point is a popular model older car and the caliber of the hunting rifle. As for Juno and Dom, they were killed with a nine millimeter handgun, so there may be no connection between the two incidents.'

Westmoreland bobbed his head and returned to the death of his son. 'I was told Dom and Juno had been spending a lot of cash lately.'

'Yes, at least a couple thousand dollars that we know of.'

'The police report said their cell phones and computer were missing.'

Gloria replied in the affirmative. 'The entire apartment had been ransacked, as if the killer was looking for something.'

'Do we know what that might have been about?'

'No. The killer or killers might have thought the boys were hiding money or drugs in the house. We really don't know.'

'You were acquainted with my son, weren't you?' the judge inquired.

'I saw him in the hallways and occasionally

when he dumped the trash, that sort of thing. He seemed like a good kid.'

'How much did he earn in his position as janitor?'

'I believe the pay was ten to twelve dollars an hour. I could check if you like, but it's within the normal range for that position.'

He was thoughtful for a moment. 'Did you check their bank accounts?'

'Dominick and Juno had both recently deposited several hundred dollars in their checking accounts,' Gloria said. 'The detectives think they might have done a drug deal or two.'

'Not my son,' Westmoreland said firmly. 'Dom used some milder drugs on occasion, usually marijuana, but he knew better than to buy and sell drugs for profit.'

'Then we are at a loss as to where the two boys got the money.'

'What about Juno?'

'We've talked to his sister, his parents and his cousin. All of them claim Juno wasn't into anything illegal either. Victor didn't force him to be part of the gang, because Juno was going to attend a technical college in the fall. He wanted to be a mechanic.'

'Do we think this hit was a warning or revenge directed at Victor?'

'It's a possibility. We're still gathering information.'

'How about the two girls who were seen leaving his and Juno's place?'

'The police are tracking them down. We think we know who they were.'

'Who is heading up the task force?'

'Captain Mercer. His top detectives, Louis Grady and Deroy Hampton are running the overall investigation.'

The judge finally turned around. His eyes were red and he blinked to prevent shedding any tears. He looked like a man who hadn't slept in two days . . . and he probably hadn't.

'You needn't be in chambers today,' Gloria said gently. 'Your family probably needs you.'

'The kids already helped to arrange the funeral and services for my son. As for going home, it is a grim reminder of the mistakes I made with Dominick. It's easier for me here.'

'Then you should lie down on the couch and try and get some rest. I assure you, we're doing everything we can to find your son's killer.'

'Thank you, Gloria. I appreciate your support and concern.'

With nothing left to say, Gloria bid farewell to the judge and left him to grieve on his own. Once into the hallway she had to stem her own tears.

Damn you, Chock Lincoln! Why did you have to kill those two boys!

* * *

Jason debarked from the airline a few minutes before 4:00 p.m. Utah time. He passed through Security and immediately experienced a stir of excitement at seeing Kari waiting for him.

The months of being absent and only hearing her voice on the telephone or reading her letters, melted away instantly. She was every bit as attractive as he remembered . . . even more so. Her sandy blond hair was loose about her shoulders, with a neatly cropped row of bangs decorating her forehead. Her cute-as-a-pixie face was flush and vibrant, and the most kissable mouth he'd ever encountered was fixed in a smile of greeting. He wondered if she had purposely dressed to rekindle his memory, having donned the same outfit as when he had first seen her. The dress was black silk and chiffon, sleeveless, with a slightly scooped neckline and snug above the waist so it flattered her trim figure. She had a jacket draped over one arm, as it was mid-March and the weather was often on the wet and cold side.

'Jason!' she shouted gleefully, unnecessarily

raising and waving her free hand so that he would spot her.

He had pondered what he would do upon seeing her again, how he ought to react. Should he be reserved, formal, bold . . . ? But the choice was made for him. Kari flew into his arms and she hugged him tightly. When she looked up at him, eyes shining as brightly as polished brass under a bright light, he did what came naturally — he kissed her.

The young woman returned the kiss, endearingly, yet withholding passion. It was a warm welcome . . . a very warm welcome.

'You're more stunning than I remembered,' he praised, rising up to gaze down at her face. 'And you must be freezing in that summer gown.'

Kari laughed. 'The weather is supposed to be warmer than usual this week, and you told me how much you liked this dress when we met at your Aunt Sally's place.'

'Devastated is the more appropriate adjective that comes to mind,' he replied. 'Angels would pale beside you.'

The statement of adulation increased the vibrancy of Kari's features, but she curbed her excitement. 'Did you have a good trip?'

'I had the misfortune of being trapped between two human snoring machines on the London flight. The jaunt from Chicago to here was better, although the flight steward kept popping off with 'G'day mate' whenever he walked past.'

'It's because you look so manly,' Kari teased. 'You know Hollywood is crazy about Australians. They think it's the only place on the planet where there are any real men left.'

'Take a look at the blooming telly and it's easy to see why,' Jason replied. 'I swear there are more men crying and sobbing on screen than women and children combined these days.'

'That's why I'm a fan of classic movies. I still like films where the guy is the one doing the saving.' She added a bit shyly, 'And I've always preferred to have the love scene fade out after they kiss.'

Jason chuckled. 'Therein is part of the reason I was attracted to you from the off.'

'Speaking of off, Jason, baggage claim is this way. Let's pick up your luggage and be off.' She took hold of his hand and began to walk.

'You should have called me,' Jason reprimanded her. 'Reggie told me you didn't want me to know about the shooting.'

'It could have been a mistake.'

'And you could have been killed,' Jason responded in a scolding tone of voice. 'What mischief are you into that might warrant such an attack?'

'Nothing at all,' Kari answered. 'It has to be a mistake or a random shooting.'

'What precautions are you taking?'

'I've been using my friend's car. Mine is getting a new windshield installed. No one knows what I'm driving except for her.'

'And the police? What have they found?'

'Nothing, other than the two bullets, I'm afraid. It's all a mystery.'

They recovered Jason's two suitcases and were on their way to the parking garage when he asked about the double murder she had reported on in the newspaper.

'The police think Juno was the target, as his cousin runs the toughest street gang in the valley.' She continued: 'But the more serious problem is the young man killed along with Juno. Dominick is the son of one of the most prominent judges in all of Utah. Judge Westmoreland won't be satisfied until the case is solved.'

Jason was incredulous. 'Someone must be short by a few shingles to kill a judge's son. What was he doing with a gang member?'

She told him about how the two boys had grown up as friends and the trouble the judge's son had been in with the police. 'Of course, no charges were ever brought against

Dominick. With his father holding such a high position, the problems always went away quietly.'

'Until now.'

'Yes, being shot and killed is definitely beyond the aid or influence of his father.'

'How deeply involved are you in the case? Could that be why someone took a shot at you?'

'I don't know, Jason.' Her reply was completely honest. But then she displayed a deep concern and asked, 'How did you get time off to come for a visit? You've been telling me that you wouldn't have any paid leave for another three months.'

'I took time off to come here and do what I could to help and protect you.'

She smiled. 'Not that I don't love the idea of having you here, but how long can you stay?'

'I intend to stay until we find out who shot at you.'

Kari pulled face. 'What if we don't find the shooter?'

'Then I'll make a nuisance of myself until the police get so tired of me they will be forced to uncover the man responsible.'

Kari laughed, a wonderfully musical mirth. 'Had I known all it took was a couple of bullets and a ruined windshield to get you back over here, I would have hired it done myself months ago!'

Reggie was outside his apartment building to meet them when Jason and Kari parked the car. He approached, all smiles, and shook Jason's hand. Next, he apologized to Kari for calling Jason.

She begrudgingly let him off without a scolding. 'I'm glad to have him here, although I can't imagine how his boss feels about him deserting his duties.'

Reggie arched his brows. 'He didn't give them a choice,' he declared. 'Jason said he was coming here to watch over you and that was that. Period!'

Kari stared at Jason. 'You didn't?!'

'Reggie makes it sound a bit more forceful than what actually happened. It's not like I threatened to quit my job or something.'

'It definitely falls into the *or something* category,' Kari countered. 'What if you lose your job over this?'

Jason dismissed the notion. 'My DCI is not so blinkered as to give me the boot for taking leave without proper notice.'

'DCI?' Reggie wondered. 'Is that like a chief of police?'

'Detective Chief Inspector,' Jason answered. 'He's the unlucky man who has to explain to the DSL our Superintendent, as to why I've gone absent.'

'See what you did?' Kari stated once more, regarding Reggie with a look of censure. 'I didn't want Jason doing something rash.'

'Yes, well, it's a little late to worry about that,' Reggie said defensively. 'He's here now.' Then, turning his attention to Jason. 'How about we toss your luggage in the apartment and the three of us can go get something to eat?'

'Sounds good to me,' Kari approved of the idea. 'I missed lunch today so I'm starved.'

'I'm adrift as to what day of the week it is,' Jason admitted. 'After an all night flight, I'll be lucky to stay awake during the meal.'

Reggie laughed. 'You let us worry about that. Kari and me are happy enough to have you here that we can keep you awake and the conversation going.'

'Jolly good,' Jason agreed.

'Yes,' Kari said, flashing Jason a flirtatious wink that about unraveled his socks. 'It's jolly marvelous!'

★ ★ ★

Hector Gomez dropped off his two pals at the clubhouse and turned his car for his girlfriend's house. Jesse Ventura, top dog of the 39th Street Lobos, had warned everyone to stay close to other gang members. The truce between them and the Hard Corps was still in effect, but he wanted everyone to be careful.

Hector had scoffed at the warning. Why get juiced up and crazy over one of Victor's banger boys getting shot? The Lobos had no beef with the mutts over on the west side. So long as they stayed off of their turf, and vice versa, neither gang had reason to worry.

He stopped at the light on 7th Street and reached over to turn up the volume on his bass audio system. The rear mounted subwoofers kicked in and the entire car vibrated to the loud rap music. Hector became aware of a car pulling alongside, but paid it no mind as it was in the turning lane. He bobbed his head in time with the music and straightened up. The light turned green . . .

A burst of gunfire from a semi-automatic weapon blew out the driver's side window and Hector's upper body was riddled with several bullets. One hit him in the temple and he slumped over the wheel, foot on the gas pedal.

The car surged forward wildly, crossed the street at an angle and slammed into a lamppost on the corner. Other cars had pulled up on the cross-streets, but the interest of the occupants were riveted on the wrecked car. Steam erupted from the damaged radiator, and the engine and the blaring music both ground to a stop. No one paid attention to the car that had been in the turning lane. It made a U-turn and disappeared into traffic.

'Call the police!' someone called out, as they approached the car.

'Better make that the coroner,' said another, looking through the shattered window. 'This guy is dead!'

8

Jason had been lethargic from the long hours of travel. He went home with Reggie after the three of them had had dinner. He had kissed Kari and apologized for being so worn out. They made plans to spend the next day together.

However, the next morning Kari was not even out of bed when the phone rang. Rather than it being Jason, it was Marge Taylor.

'You'd better tell your English suitor to have a cup of tea and cool his jets for a little while longer, Kari.'

'I put in for vacation today,' Kari complained. 'I haven't had any time off since — '

'We have another gang death.' Marge cut her off. 'This was one of the 39th Street Lobos. It may be retaliation for Victor's cousin.'

Kari caught her breath. 'This could mean a gang war!'

'Yes, and I wanted to give you the chance to cover it, seeing as how you did the piece on Juno and Dominick. If you would prefer, I can hand it off to Charise or — '

'No!' Kari stopped her from continuing. 'I'll handle it.'

'The police chief is supposed to give a statement in a little over an hour. We need to cover the briefing.'

'Soon as I'm dressed I'll head over to the station and take notes.'

'You'll need to write the article, so you better come into the office,' Marge advised. 'Once Scott approves your piece, I'll try and get you out of here.'

Kari sighed. 'All right. I'll call Jason and let him know. I'll see you after the briefing.'

Marge said goodbye and Kari immediately punched in another phone number. Reggie was the one who answered. Jason was in the shower, so Kari told Reggie about the murder and the need to go in to work for a few hours. She promised to call Jason as soon as she knew when she would be free for the day.

Rushing about, Kari skipped breakfast, threw on her clothes, then hastily applied a touch of makeup and brushed out her hair. She was on the road in minutes and arrived shortly after the film crews from the local TV networks had set up for the briefing. She had to take a corner spot and hoped she could hear what was being said.

Captain Mercer was the one who spoke. He was brief and took only a couple questions. At the end it was clear that the police knew nothing of consequence. Yes, this could have been a retaliation for Juno's death, but it might have been a fight over drugs, a girl, or even a random attack. And no, they had no further information to share concerning the deaths of Juno and Dominick.

Kari arrived at her desk and began to write the story. It sorely lacked details, but so did the police. She could only speculate that there might be a connection to the killing of a gang member from a rival group.

Kari worked over several different drafts and was nearly finished when a shadow fell over her chair. She glanced up to see Dee standing there. Her friend had two cups of coffee and a plate with two donuts.

'I'm sure last night's entertainment culminated in a good morning romp, so I know you didn't have a chance to eat.'

'I got home early and went to bed . . . alone.' Then she reached out and took the cup of coffee. 'However, I did miss my morning caffeine.'

Dee set down her cup and the saucer, then groaned in melodramatic fashion, 'Kari, Kari, where did I go wrong?' She sat down next to her and gave a solemn shake of her head. 'Haven't I taught you yet about the fun of having dessert after your meal?'

'I haven't seen Jason for several months. And . . . ' Kari hesitated, 'well, you know, we have never been completely intimate.'

'Here I was, thinking Jason was cut in the mold of another James Bond, the quintessential Brit.'

'Jason informed me that all people within the British Commonwealth are Brits, while he is from England. That makes him English and a Brit.'

'All right, you're a Utahan American and he's an English Brit. You're avoiding the point.' She held out her clenched hands like a plea for understanding. 'Love is universal, kiddo. It doesn't matter if he's a Brit, a Yank or a three-legged alien. You've got to have some adventure and romance in your life. When do you get to the good stuff?'

'If it's meant to be, we'll get there.'

Dee uttered a noisy sigh of disappointment. 'I hope you'll still be young enough to enjoy it.'

'I'm leaving as soon as I get this approved,' Kari informed her. 'Thanks for the coffee, but I'm going to have lunch with Jason in a short while.'

'Thanks a heap,' Dee complained. 'That means I eat double my pastry allotment for the day. Do you have any idea what you're doing to my calorie intake?'

'Offer one to Marge,' Kari suggested with a wry grin. 'Maybe a show of kinship would get you moved into a corner office.'

Dee snipped haughtily. 'Thanks for nothing, kiddo. The corner office is the janitor's closet!'

★ ★ ★

After a couple hours alone at Reggie's apartment, Jason decided to take the light rail and meet Kari at the *Sentinel* office. She had rung him up and said she would be free shortly after noon. As he had plenty of time, he decided to visit the parking garage and look over the scene of the sniper shooting.

A uniform was still in the area, questioning passers-by if they had seen anything on the day of the shooting. Jason talked to him and discovered what little the officer knew.

'So the police think the shots were to scare her?' he asked, once he had learned what he could.

'Both shots hit the passenger side of the windshield,' the cop replied confidently. 'If he'd have been trying to kill her, he'd have aimed for the driver's side of the car.'

'What time did the shooting occur?'

'About . . . ' the cop looked at his watch, 'thirty minutes from now. The shooting was reported at a quarter to twelve.'

Jason thanked the man and walked over to stand out of the way of the ramp. He watched as several cars left, and studied the building across the way. The shots had been fired from the roof.

Kari said she had stopped to check traffic and was squinting because of the bright sunlight. That made sense, as she had just come from a dark garage, but still . . .

Considering the area, the distance and angle of the shoot, it was obvious the man behind the rifle was experienced. He had used a .308 caliber weapon, a hunting rifle with the power to knock down either deer or elk. That meant the bullet would not glance off the glass as sometimes happened with a smaller-caliber gun.

The two boys were killed with a 9 millimeter handgun, three deadly kill shots for each victim. This was no amateur shooter. Most gang killings were haphazard with bullets flying everywhere. From what Kari had told him, this was a single shooter and he was very accurate and cool about the executions.

It was certainly possible that the man had purposely fired into the passenger side of the car. Then again, Jason didn't feel like dismissing the shots as mere scare tactics.

Hampton held up the report. 'No witnesses to the crime, other than a dark-colored car seen pulling away from Hector's vehicle. No one got a good look, because they were focused on Hector smashing into the lamppost.'

'Any traffic cameras up there?' Grady asked.

'The one at the intersection wasn't working. We need to get lucky before this gang thing escalates into a full-scale war.'

'Speaking of getting lucky,' Grady remarked with a smirk. 'Peggy was real cheerful when I passed her in the hallway yesterday.'

Hampton was immediately wary. 'She's a very upbeat kind of gal.'

'Funny, but it's the first time she ever smiled at me all friendly like.' At Hampton's scowl, Grady continued to tease him. 'You two getting together has done wonders for both of your personalities.'

'You keep pushing my buttons, Grady,' Hampton warned, 'and I'll tell your wife that you've been having desserts for lunch again.'

That sobered his partner. 'Hey! Don't be doing something like that. She and I have been taking walks most every evening to stay fit.'

'Yeah, well, she'll *have* a fit if she learns about the apple turnover you ate yesterday and the piece of cake the day before that.'

'All right, Ham,' he growled. 'If you're going to get nasty about it, I'll stop badgering you about your girlfriend.'

Hampton guffawed in an annoying manner. 'I always knew who wore the pants in your family.'

'Grab your hat, big mouth,' Grady replied tersely. 'We've got an interview with Jesse Ventura, aka El Hefe of the 39th Street Lobos.'

'You sure know how to make a guy's day,' Hampton complained. 'We get to talk to the head honchos from the two biggest gangs in town all in the same week. It doesn't get any better, does it?'

'Got to stop this feud before it gets out of hand. You want to be lead this time?'

'He's your meat, Grady. It's your turn to be called all of the pig names.' Hampton grinned. 'At least, a good many of those will be in Spanish.'

'Right,' his partner replied. 'I can pretend I didn't take three years of Spanish in school. It always twists their tails a little when we force them to use English insults.'

* * *

102

'This isn't what we signed up for!' Gloria barked at Tony. 'What does Lincoln think he's doing — starting a war?'

'I didn't know he was going to go after one of the Lobos or shoot anybody else,' Tony lamented. 'I swear, the only thing I told him was to scare the reporter and then break into her house and steal whatever he wanted.'

'Another murder,' Gloria seethed. 'This is a nightmare.'

'It isn't my fault, Glory honey. I talked to him on the phone this morning and he said he didn't want a bunch of bangers looking for him for the rest of his life.'

'What about this second killing?' she cried. 'Is he expecting us to pay him more money for something we didn't ask for?'

'No,' Tony promised her. 'He opened fire at Hector so this would look like a gang retaliation. It was to cover his own butt.'

Gloria pounded a fist into her palm. 'We've created a monster! That man is completely out of control.'

'It's over and done with now,' Tony promised. 'Once Lincoln ransacks the Underwood place, we're done with him.'

'Unless someone starts looking at him for these killings,' she contradicted. 'I don't trust him.' She pinned Tony with a hard stare, her teeth bared in a sneer. 'How much did you tell him? What all does he know . . . about us?'

'Nothing!' Tony whimpered. 'I gave him the money and our instructions. He didn't hook up the computer or check out the phones, and he didn't find any photos stashed in the apartment. He only took the cash from Dom's and Juno's wallets so this would look like a gang hit or robbery.'

'At least that part makes sense.'

Tony squeaked like a mouse. 'This is it . . . right?'

'Almost.' She didn't hide her anxiety. 'Soon as he burgles Underwood's place, we're finished.'

'Maybe there is a positive side to this,' Tony offered. 'I mean, if the gangs start shooting at one another, it will take the heat off of our problem.'

'I didn't want blood on my hands over this! I'd rather have let Don take half of everything I own.'

'He hasn't said anything about divorce, has he?'

'No.' She uttered a cynical grunt. 'Don's only got half a brain. He still thinks we're both partners in a private world of marital bliss.'

'Then we don't have to worry.'

'We have to worry if those pictures show up!' she snapped. 'Plus, we've got an entire police force looking for a killer — the very man we hired!'

'You'll figure a way to get that taken care of,' Tony assured her. 'You're smarter than the Neanderthals out there beating the pavement. Besides, no one has been able to ID Lincoln. He has not been seen, except at a distance, and the reporter can't even offer a description of him.'

'There's still one major problem, Tony,' Gloria told him. 'I didn't find the photos.' She dug her nails into her palms. 'There was nothing on the phones and the laptop was clean, other than for a couple of porn sites. We can be thankful one of those two idiots didn't post our pictures on the web for the world to see.'

'So where are the pictures?'

Gloria made a helpless gesture. 'Who can say? Either they deleted them after I paid the money or they used a storage device like a flash drive. I don't think they would have given the photos to anyone else.'

'I'll bet they destroyed them after they got their money.'

'Of course,' Gloria was sarcastic, 'everyone knows how truthful and honest blackmailers are.'

Tony wrung his hands, his voice whiny again. 'But . . . ' he tried to put a positive spin on the situation, 'but if no one else contacts us about ransom for the pictures . . . ? Well, that would mean we're in the clear, wouldn't it?'

Gloria took a deep breath and let it out slowly. She had to maintain control. Lincoln was supposedly done causing havoc; there had been no further blackmail threats and the reporter didn't have a clue as to why someone had shot at her. 'I suppose we might be safe,' she finally allowed.

Tony straightened up and a guarded smile spread across his face. He was like a pet again, a big, loveable Labrador. Discipline the dog and it would sorrowfully hang its head. An instant later it would approach its owner meekly again, eyes beseeching, tail wagging, wanting to move past the scolding and get a pat on the head.

Gloria resisted the urge to give this dog a swift kick to the groin for these past major screw-ups. It would have made her feel better. But Tony had a fragile ego. He needed reinforcement to act like a man. He had always gotten that kind of support from his wife. Rather than have him go shuffling back to her, Gloria took the higher road.

'How about the guns Lincoln used?'

'I have them both.' Tony gave her a helpless

shrug. 'Had to pay Lincoln five hundred dollars to get them. Took everything I had from my bank account.'

Another oath under her breath. 'I hope to heaven we didn't exchange one blackmailer for another.'

'I told him we were done,' Tony said. 'Lincoln is guilty of three murders and would likely get a death sentence if he gets caught. Plus, I never told him what kind of pictures he was searching for. Without knowing our motive, he can't point his finger at us. If he did, we could laugh at the absurdity of any accusations.'

'All right.' Gloria returned to future business. 'To sell the notion that this is a gang war, it would help if we could plant the rifle on the Lobos and the pistol he used for Hector on the Hard Corps.'

'As a Deputy District Attorney in the investigation, I can arrange to be on hand during the execution of any search warrant. Once the police have a few suspects and get a court order or two, I'll see the weapons are found and traced back to the right people.'

'Just make sure there are no prints from Lincoln or yourself on the weapons.'

Tony's facial features tightened noticeably. 'I started hunting with my father when I was fourteen. I know how to handle a weapon.'

Gloria didn't apologize. In a dismissive tone, she said, 'Whatever.' Then she concluded, 'The sooner we get this done the better.'

9

Once Kari was finished at work, she and Jason walked to the new City Creek Mall in downtown Salt Lake City. They had a light lunch at the café court and browsed at the numerous shops and water exhibits. To finish off the afternoon they spent an hour on the guided tour of the Utah State Capitol building.

Back at Kari's apartment, Kari had a surprise for Jason. She set the tea kettle on the stove and then removed a familiar looking package of tea from the cupboard.

'I did some research online,' Kari explained. 'Took me a few telephone calls and I had to drive up to the east side to get it, but I wanted you to feel at home.'

Jason smiled at her effort. 'PG Tips is the brand of tea I drink most often. This is very thoughtful of you.'

Kari asked, 'Chinese cuisine all right with you tonight?'

'Fine. I like almost everything on the menu.'

Kari punched in a number and gave an order. Then she got two coffee cups and placed them on the small dining table.

'If you don't mind, I'd like to take a shower before we eat.'

'That's fine. I'll ring up Reggie and leave a message not to expect me until late.'

The order of fried rice, egg rolls, sesame chicken and chow mein arrived before Kari had finished her shower. Jason, having changed a sizable amount of English currency for American money, paid the delivery person.

He did a brew up with the PG Tips so the tea was ready by the time Kari came into the kitchen. He paused to drink in the subtle beauty of the woman. She had touched up her light makeup and kept her hair dry, although there was a hint of moisture along her bangs. She wore a casual pink blouse, with a modest V-neck, and a pleated white skirt that was about knee length. As was her habit when at her apartment, she wore no shoes.

'I might have warned you that I have excellent timing when it comes to paying for deliveries,' she teased.

'Yes, I would have taken the money from your purse, but I doubted I could get it sorted before the food was cold.'

'A woman's purse is her private labyrinth.' She made an impish face. 'It's part of our allure.'

Jason laughed his agreement and she took a seat opposite him at the table. After taking a taste of the tea, she said, 'Umm, I think I'm developing a taste for this. Two sugars and a dash of cream?'

'As your taste matures, you'll likely cut back on the sugar.'

'Ah, yes,' she joked. 'Now that I've succumbed to English tea, I'll soon acquire a more sophisticated taste.'

'Quite,' he replied.

They engaged in light conversation while dining. As Kari began to clear the table, Jason took note of a pile of papers on Kari's desk.

'It appears you still do a lot of your work at home. What do you have on the murders?'

'Not a lot.' She explained everything that had happened concerning the two young men, the shots fired at her car and the death of the gang member from the 39th Street Lobos. She also told him about the strange man she had seen parked near Juno's and Dom's rented house. 'There are no suspects other than the unknown man,' she finished.

'But you got nothing out of your interview?'

'I wrote down what I could remember, but it was all gibberish.'

'Anything might help.'

Kari removed the notebook from her

purse. She flipped the page and found the few notes she had jotted down during and after the meeting. 'I tried to rewrite the sentences as best I could, but they were full of silly, useless stuff.'

Jason looked at the page, studied it for a moment, shook his head and agreed. 'It does look like nonsense.'

Once the few dishes were cleaned and put away, Kari put ice and Pepsi into two glasses and placed them on the coffee table next to the loveseat. Jason took a seat, while she switched on some soft background music, lighted a couple scented candles and then turned out the lights.

He raised his arm as she came over and joined him. After a few moments, they shared a kiss and warm embrace. Kari leaned back afterwards and murmured, 'I imagine this seems rather schoolgirlish, but this is the ritual I use when we talk on the phone. I have candles and music and pretend you're here with me.'

Jason gazed at her for a long moment, stroked her silken hair, then uttered a despondent sigh.

'What is it?' Kari asked, frowning an immediate concern.

'I don't know how to explain it.'

She sat up straight and studied him with

her rich brown eyes. 'You can try. I'm not as thick as some.'

He grinned at her English expression. 'I'm afraid I might be the one who is thick. I want to hold you, kiss you . . . ' his voice became gentle, 'do more than that.'

'But?' she coaxed.

'I would hate myself forever if I hurt you.'

Kari traced the tips of her fingers along his cheek. 'I don't believe you would ever hurt me.'

'Not intentionally,' Jason said, gazing deeply into her eyes. 'But we do have a rather complex relationship. When I met you, you were my cousin Roger's girlfriend. You didn't even have time to get over his cruel betrayal before we were . . . involved.'

'Roger Cline is not part of our lives any more,' Kari disregarded his concern, utterly enraptured by his smoky grey eyes. 'We got past him before you left. Reggie understands about how his brother treated women. He's perfectly OK with you and me being together. Your aunt Sally and even my folks have accepted we are a couple, so the hard part is over.'

'No, the hard part is that I happen to reside on the other side of the ocean. Once I'm convinced you are safe, I'll be leaving again.'

'We can find a way around that,' she

persisted. 'What else is bothering you?'

Jason lifted one shoulder in a shrug. 'I suppose I still feel a measure of guilt for not being faithful to Doris.'

'You told me that Doris wanted you to find another person to love.'

'Yes, but it isn't that easy. I do want to move on, but it's difficult.'

'Maybe you really don't care for me?'

'No!' he stated adamantly. 'That is absolutely not part of the problem.'

'Then what else matters?'

'A proper courtship between two people is more than a visit every six months. I would feel like a proper heel if we escalated our relationship when there isn't any future for us.'

'You're talking about one of us having to give up their career and move across the ocean. That's really what you're saying, isn't it?'

Jason rested his hands on her shoulders, consumed by the desire to hold Kari close and never let her go. But the future offered an impossible choice. Could she leave the position she had worked for for so long and hard and move to England? Could he leave his position with the CID and start a new life in America?

Kari leaned forward and gently touched his

114

lips with her own. When she drew back, she whispered, 'If we truly love each other, we'll find a way, Jason.'

'Two demanding careers in a relationship almost never works,' he argued softly.

She slipped inside his guard, arms going about his neck, and subtly rotated around on to his lap. 'I don't want to lose you, Jason,' she murmured, her lips only inches from his own. 'I've fallen in love with you.'

Jason knew in his heart that he would never find another woman like Kari. When she kissed him a second time, he surrendered to his desire and kissed her right back.

★ ★ ★

The captain stood at Grady's desk, hands on his hips and an unhappy look on his face.

'Are we any closer to finding anyone of interest in these murders?'

'I'm afraid not, Capt'n,' Grady replied. 'Ventura claims the Lobos had nothing to do with Dom and Juno's deaths. But he is looking for payback for Hector being killed.'

'Oh, we're in a great position. Two of the biggest gangs in the valley are out for each other's blood. We're sitting on a bomb, gentlemen.' He glanced from Grady to Hampton. 'It could go off at any minute and tear this city apart.'

Hampton harrumphed under his intense stare and offered up a little news. 'We tracked down the blue Ford Taurus the reporter saw outside Juno's place. It had the dent in the front fender, exactly the way she described it.'

'And?'

'It had been stolen from an autobody shop. One of the employees left the keys in it overnight. They didn't report it because they assumed the owner had needed the car and picked it up.'

'What about prints?'

'It was wiped clean. We have it over at Impound and are still going over it, but nothing so far,'

'How about a motive for these murders?'

'It doesn't appear to have been linked to the visit of the two girls,' Hampton reported. 'Lana Monroe used to hang with Victor, but claims there were no hard feelings about their breakup. The other girl is a friend of Lana's and was just out for a good time. Lana said Dom became what she termed as 'overly aggressive' after a drink or two and they left.'

'Sounds like Dom,' Grady inserted. 'He had a reputation for being abusive towards women.'

'So what else could this be about?' The captain was growing desperate.

'It possibly has something to do with the big monthly drug shipment that comes in from Colombia. You remember the piece Kari Underwood did after those people were chased out of the hills by men watching over a field of marijuana. Well, we believe the reason for shooting at the reporter was because she showed up at just the wrong time and gave the impression that she knew something.'

'But she doesn't know anything . . . right?'

'She's totally without a clue,' Grady answered. 'We're guessing one of the drug lords is paranoid and got the wrong idea from her visit.'

'What about stealing the phones and computer? What was the killer looking for in Dom and Juno's place?'

'No way to tell,' Hampton said. 'We've tried to backtrack the extra money those two had been flashing around, but we've hit a stone wall. Other than their regular pay-checks, their bank deposits were in cash, as were their last few purchases for the television and Xbox . . . even the games and DVDs. Whatever they were into, they were getting paid in cash.'

'But it wasn't for dealing dope?'

'Not according to the street informants and the gang unit. I checked with Rick Cory

— our most knowledgeable cop on the streets.'

'Cory is a good man,' the captain agreed. 'Before he took over we had a lot more drive-bys and other shootings, with a good many innocent people getting injured or killed. He's done a lot of good by negotiating peace between the gangs.'

'And he has the best source around,' Grady added quickly.

Hampton summarized, 'Even so, he couldn't offer any help on these murders. To his knowledge, Juno and Dom were never involved in drugs, other than to buy a small amount of marijuana for their own kicks. And Hector was a small fish in the pond.'

'Does he have any idea that might fit?'

'No,' Grady responded. 'He reported that no one on the streets seems to know anything about the two shootings.'

'And we've had no luck finding the dealer who is trading with the Colombians?'

'Cory and the entire gang unit are in the dark. They've been trying to find the people bringing the monthly cocaine shipments for over a year, but have come up with zilch.'

'OK. Well, keep at it. Use all the resources you need.'

'You bet, Capt'n,' Grady said. 'We're still cross-checking everything from the three deaths and have added in the shots fired at the reporter.'

The captain gave an approving bob of his head. 'You two are killing my budget, logging all these man hours on a single case. But we need results before this ends up with a dozen people getting killed.'

'We're following every possible lead,' Hampton was quick to reply.

'Plus we now have the Brit back in town.' Grady was half serious. 'I wouldn't be surprised to see him show up with his own theory or idea one of these next days.'

'Thanks.' The captain didn't hide his lack of enthusiasm, 'Having an outsider on board, along with his snoopy reporter girlfriend, makes me feel so much better.'

As soon as the captain left them alone, Grady whispered, 'I wouldn't mind Keane's help. We're like a race car that's stuck in neutral. We can't even spin our wheels!'

'I hear you, partner.' Hampton heaved a sigh. 'Now, tell me you've got some inkling of what we do next.'

⋆   ⋆   ⋆

Deciding the best way to help Kari was to find out the who and why of the murders, Jason agreed they should do some

119

investigating on their own. After going over the police list of witnesses and likely suspects, they opted to visit Juno's older sister. Kari had been on her way to talk to her when the shots were fired at her car. As Rita Orozco was rumored to have been closer to Juno than anyone else in his family, she hoped the girl could offer them some helpful information.

Rita was a caregiver and companion for a moderately wealthy elderly woman. The lady's residence was an older home, in a nicely cared for area, a short way from the Hogle Zoo. They arrived to discover Juno's sister unloading some groceries from the trunk of a 2008 black Cadillac CTS. Also in the driveway was a brand-new copper-coloured Volvo sedan.

Kari introduced herself and Jason offered to carry in the remaining packages.

Rita was fairly attractive, an inch or two shorter than Kari's five-foot-four inch height. She had a woman's build, and her black hair was well down over her shoulders. Her clothes were much nicer than those of most girls in the homecare field, with a designer purse slung over one shoulder.

'Weekly shopping,' Rita explained to them. 'Ms Lovendaul doesn't often leave the house.'

'You've a nice car,' Jason said, admiring the Volvo.

Rita smiled. 'It's got everything, including a big monthly payment and sky-high insurance.'

'We would like to talk to you about Juno.' Kari explained the purpose of their visit. 'Do you have a minute?'

'Let me put the groceries away first. Ms Lovendaul is always concerned about keeping her produce fresh.'

'Lead the way,' Jason offered, picking up the final two sacks and then closing the trunk of the Caddy.

Ms Lovendaul seemed happy for some company. She also took a shine to Jason, as soon as she heard him speak.

'Australian, aren't you?' she guessed.

'English, actually,' Jason replied, masking his normal frustration.

'Let me show you my house,' the woman insisted. 'I've had a lot of work done lately. It's all so very nice.'

'Certainly,' Jason replied politely, setting the sacks on the table for Rita. 'I can see the place is adequately maintained.'

Kari noticed a slight crease appear along Rita's forehead, as if she wasn't happy to have her employer showing a stranger around the house. She discarded the notion as being overly protective and began questioning the girl while she was putting away the grocery items.

'I've been told you and your brother were quite close,' she began.

'Juno and I were the last kids at home, you know? We had six brothers and sisters who had moved out by the time we were in junior high. Me and Juno pretty much depended on each other right up through high school. Our folks were getting along in years, so we had to do a lot for them.'

'And Dominick was your brother's best friend?'

Rita had been putting some items in the refrigerator. She paused from the chore giving the simple question some thought.

'Look, I know you and the cops think those two were into something bad, selling drugs or the like. It's not true. As for Dom and Juno being best of friends, I liked Dom, but I wouldn't have let my worst enemy go out on a date with him.'

'I read about his run-ins with the police about battering a girl or two.'

'He changed after his mother died. It's like he kind of hated her for leaving him and took it out on every girl he dated . . . know what I mean?'

'I think so.'

'No matter what kind of animal he was around women, he wasn't a thief or drug dealer. Dom and my brother never got involved with that stuff. Juno was going to get some technical training in auto mechanics and start his own garage. Dom was going to work with him, keeping the books and handling the money. They had plans for a future, Miss Underwood. They wanted to make something out of their lives.'

'They seemed to have come into some money lately,' Kari said.

Rita returned to the chore of storing the produce items. 'Last time I talked to Juno, he said they were doing some odd jobs for people, building stuff or installing carpet, things like that.'

'You're sure it was nothing illegal?'

'Yes,' Rita stated emphatically, closing the refrigerator door harder than necessary. 'It had nothing to do with gangs, or dealing drugs, or breaking the law.'

Jason returned a few moments later with Ms Lovendaul. 'It's a big, beautiful house,' he praised to Kari and Rita. 'It's plain to see why she needs help taking care of it.'

The elderly woman beamed. 'Rita helps me with everything I need,' she said. 'The girl's been like a guardian angel to me.'

'You're too kind, Ida,' Rita replied,

beaming a smile at her. 'I'm happy to have found such a wonderful lady to look after.'

'We won't take any more of your time,' Kari said. 'It was very nice of you to speak to us.'

'You kids feel free to come back any time,' Ms Lovendaul invited. 'We can have coffee next time.'

They thanked both of them for their hospitality and returned to the car. Once on the street, Kari told Jason what Rita had said about her brother and Dom.

'Yes, Ms Lovendaul had nothing but praise for Rita. She is lonely but sound of mind. There has been a lot of work done to fix up the house lately, minor repairs, a new sink and storage shed, that sort of thing.'

'Rita is convinced Juno and Dom were not involved in any drug dealing and said they had been doing work on the side for their extra money. That leaves us with robbery as the only motive.'

'Unless a boyfriend or father of one of the girls Dom abused came calling,' Jason suggested.

'I have the name of the last girl Dom assaulted. We'll check with her next.'

'Sounds like a good idea.'

'Oh, Dee called me before you arrived this morning. Her daughter is getting married next month and they are having a bridal shower for her tonight. I hate to — '

'It's fine,' Jason cut her explanation short. 'Reggie said his grandfather, Tynan, would like to go shoot some pool tonight. I was going to ask if you wanted to tag along.'

'Not that Tynan isn't a fun character, and I do like Reggie, but this works out better for both of us. Dee is my best friend at work and I promised her ages ago that I would help with the party.'

'I'll ring up Reggie and let him know there will only be the three of us tonight.'

Kari glanced at her watch. 'After we see this next person, we can stop for lunch.' She smiled at Jason. 'I don't want anything too filling as I'm taking you to one of my favorite restaurants tonight.'

'Are you certain we will have time before your party?'

'The place I have in mind opens early for supper. We'll eat about five.'

Jason chuckled. 'Might as well spend our time eating. It's not as if we're setting the Thames on fire with our investigation.'

Kari threw him an inquisitive glance. 'I don't know what the Thames has to do with anything, but I'm ready to eat something.'

10

Grady and Hampton kept the two men separated, one to either side of the interview table. Victor Orozco had spouted off a string of vile names and refused to sit down. He stood with his tattooed arms folded and glared across at the leader of the 39th Street Lobos, Jesse Ventura. Returning the baleful stare, Jesse glowered back; neither of them had yet uttered a word to the other.

'Now you two listen up!' Hampton's voice boomed within the closed room. 'We don't want a bloody war in the valley. If there's one more incident linked to either of you, we'll round up all of the members of both of your gangs and toss you all in jail!'

'We didn't draw first blood,' Victor said between clenched teeth.

Jesse opened up. 'Your flunkies killed Hector!'

'I never gave the order,' Victor snarled back. 'If someone wasted Hector, it wasn't on my order!'

'Same goes for Juno!' Jesse fired back. 'Why would one of my guys take out a no-account like him? What would there be to gain?'

'Maybe you thought he knew something,' Victor surmised. 'Maybe you are the ones dealing with the Colombians?'

'We ain't looking to draw fire from the feds with our enterprise,' Jesse replied. 'We prefer working under their radar.'

'No different for the Hard Corps,' Victor threw the words back at him. 'We didn't have nothing to do with Hector.'

'Unless you ain't the big dog who actually runs the Hard Corps any more,' Jesse said. 'Maybe someone is looking to move up in your gang!'

'And it could be you don't know squat about what your boys are up to either!'

'All right!' Hampton's bass voice again filled the room. 'This is why we brought the two of you together, to sort this out.'

'Ain't nothing to sort out, Porky,' Victor jeered. 'If the Lobos want a war, we'll damn well bury them all!'

'You cross into our territory or go dissing my boys and we'll see who gets burned!' Jesse fired back.

'There isn't going to be any war!' Hampton silenced them both. 'We believe this is a third party's doings, someone who wants you two to take the blame.'

Victor removed his hard glare from Jesse and looked at the detective. 'Why would anyone want us busting caps at each other?'

'To hide what is really going on.'

'And what's the real happening?' Jesse wanted to know.

Hampton was trapped. 'We don't know yet,' he said lamely. 'But . . . ' he hurried to add, 'we've got all of our resources checking this out.'

'And your resources got zip,' Victor scoffed their efforts.

Grady, who had let Hampton do the talking, now entered into the fray. 'We know there was a man watching Dom and Juno's place. We located his stolen car and figure him as probably the shooter.' As both gang leaders turned their attention to him, he continued: 'We also have a preliminary on the car used during Hector's attack. It had also been stolen and was found abandoned a mile from the intersection where Hector died.'

'Which is proof of what, dogg?'

'It's the same MO — two ganglike hits; two stolen cars; and possibly the very same man doing the shooting. It looks as if someone is trying to start a war between your two gangs.'

That caused the two bangers to rethink their positions. Victor was quicker on the uptake and directed his question to Jesse.

'What would someone have to gain by us getting down over this?'

'A dude would be hella-crazy to try something like that,' Jesse responded.

'It's what we've been trying to tell you,' Hampton advised the two men. 'This whole thing appears to be a setup, a frame job to get you both at each other's throats.' His voice mellowed and he asked, 'Can either of you think of some person or another gang who benefits from you butting heads?'

'We ain't got no beef with the Hard Corps,' Jesse said. 'They don't have nothing we want.'

'Same goes for us,' Victor agreed. 'We've always had an unspoken alliance with the Lobos. There's never been bad blood between us.'

'We're asking for you to keep the peace until we can find whoever is behind these attacks,' Grady spoke again. 'We don't want any more killing.'

'You best find the dude responsible for these murders, Mr. Policeman,' Victor sneered. 'Else me an' Ventura will do our own looking.'

'Somebody is going to pay for killing Hector,' Jesse concurred.

Hampton, satisfied the two gang leaders were not going to kill each other, opened the door. 'You two are free to go. Let us know if you think of anything that can help with our investigation.'

Victor showed a smirk. 'You'll be the first person I call.'

Jesse instilled the same cynical tone in his voice. 'Yeah, awright, Mr. Policeman. We'll put you at the top of our speed dial.'

Once the two gang leaders were gone, Grady walked over to Hampton's side and exhaled a sigh. 'I believe we might have forestalled a gang war here today.'

'For the time being,' Hampton allowed. 'We need to figure out who is behind these murders and why.'

★　★　★

Kari and Jason's efforts were fruitless. Tracking down girls connected to Dom and Juno offered no leads. They also got nothing from Dominick Westmoreland's siblings. Benjamin claimed Dom was headstrong and liked to drink, but maintained his brother was only a mild drug user. Both he and his sister, Constance, avowed Dom was a good kid except for his habit of talking trash and the way he treated girls. They had no idea why someone had killed him, and they felt the same about Juno, because he had always been a hard worker and good influence on their brother.

With little new material for an article, Kari decided they would call it a day. She drove up to 13th East and stopped at the Outback restaurant, a place boasting Australian style cuisine. The hostess greeted them with a smile and asked, 'How many for dinner tonight?'

'Just the two of us, love,' Jason responded automatically.

'Oh!' she said gleefully, practically drooling over Jason. 'Are you from Australia?'

'England!' Kari snapped, before Jason could answer, flaring up at the girl's blatant ogling. 'He's British.'

'Even better!' the hostess whispered, so as to not be overheard by other patrons. 'Brits are much more polite in public than most Aussies. I'm afraid some of *them* try to live up to those beer commercials about what it takes to be a real man.'

'Yes,' Kari stated frankly. 'Being rowdy, belching, drinking too much, and acting like a juvenile delinquent in public, is not my idea of a man.'

'I agree,' the hostess replied. 'But I do love the accent.'

Jason flinched from Kari's fingernails digging into his arm. 'Do you have a table available?' she prompted the young woman.

'Right this way,' the hostess replied, flashing her teeth and bright eyes at Jason again. Then she led them to a corner booth. 'Will this do?' she asked sweetly, turning to look at Jason.

'It's fine,' Kari answered for them. 'Thank you.'

Fortunately, another group had come in and were waiting to be seated. The hostess bid them a good evening and hurried to greet the new customers.

'I swear, Jason,' Kari complained. 'Women behave around you like construction workers do around a pretty girl. I'm not going to let you open your mouth in public from now on.'

He laughed at her display of jealousy. 'Are you telling me all out-of-country guests aren't greeted so warmly?'

Kari didn't miss a beat with her reply. 'Only the handsome ones with an *Australian* accent!'

A male waiter arrived to take their order. A hot loaf of sweet brown bread was served while they were waiting. They took the time to discuss their lack of success in finding a direction to pursue that might lead them to their killer. After agreeing the investigation was stagnant without more information, Kari outlined the evening.

'By the time we get to my place, I'll have to shower and change, then hurry to get over to Dee's for the bridal shower.'

'Reggie said he had reserved a pool table at seven o'clock as Tynan is not a night person. I imagine we will finish up our games about the time you are wrapping up your party.'

'Are you any good at billiard games?'

'Reggie and I had almost no chance when we played against Roger.'

Kari groaned. 'Is there anything that man isn't good at?'

'Well, there is a rumor that he doesn't get on with intelligent and beautiful women,' Jason said wryly.

The remark caused Kari to laugh without humor. It still smarted that she had been used by him and dumped like garbage afterwards. To hide the rush of shame she felt over their ruinous relationship, she said, 'Yes, he does have a pitiful track record when it comes to long term relationships with the opposite sex.'

'In essence, Roger is due some credit. He is the one who not only brought us together, but helped you land a job as a reporter. If he hadn't been in both of our lives, we wouldn't be together and you might still be writing death notices, awaiting a chance to display your writing talent.'

'I never thanked him properly for his boost to my career. Tell me, would my sending him a bomb count as gratitude?'

Jason laughed and Kari joined in. It was a welcome relief that the two of them were able to put Roger's treacherous behavior toward Kari into the past.

After a satisfying meal, Jason saw Kari home. He didn't offer to come in on this occasion, as each of them had plans for the night. The question of dating had been answered, but the next step had not been taken. They embraced, kissed with ardor, and parted as lovers. But the troublesome conundrum still lingered. How could they ever be a couple together?

★ ★ ★

The phone rang and Gloria's husband answered. After a moment, he said, 'It's for you, babe.'

Gloria examined Don's expression, but he gave no indication of who it was on the line. It was unsettling to hear Tony's voice on the other end.

'Mr. Martin, what's happened?' she asked, trying to sound professional.

Don wandered off toward the living room and television, apparently uninterested in her taking a business call at home.

'I wouldn't have called you, but two problems have come up.' Tony sounded nervous and out of breath.

'Tell me,' Gloria prompted. 'What kind of problems?'

'Paul Hanson is sticking his nose in our business. Somehow he discovered we had dismissed the weapons charge against Lincoln. He caught up with me as I was leaving the office and wanted to know why I had let the man off with a warning.'

Gloria suppressed an oath. 'What did you tell him?'

'That the circumstances didn't warrant his being sent back to jail. I pointed out how a minor infraction like that would cost the poor man eight years in prison.'

His excuse caused Gloria to mutter critically. 'I'm sure that satisfied him.'

Tony's voice was shaky and weak. 'I think he knows about us.'

'He doesn't *know* anything,' Gloria admonished him in a hushed voice, glancing at the hallway to the living room, concerned that Don might be able to hear. 'If Paul had some pejorative information concerning that situation, he would come to me about it. He'd like nothing better than to derail my re-election.'

'He certainly acted like he was privy to something. It was in the way he looked at me and how he talked . . . ?'

'Forget about him. Paul is always looking for an edge, anything he can use to dislodge my hold on this office. If he approaches you again, you send him to me. I know how to deal with his kind.'

'I'm worried about him,' Tony complained. 'When he spoke of you, he inserted a number of innuendos, as if he was saying one thing and meant another. I don't trust him.'

'Of course we don't trust him! He's the opposition. My opponent!' Gloria's voice had raised until the pitch filled the room. She bit down hard, gnashing her teeth, and forcibly cooled her ire.

'You said there were two problems,' she reminded Tony. 'What is the second one?'

'Ballistics just came back from Hector's murder,' Tony blurted out. 'That brain-challenged dipstick, Lincoln, used the same nine millimeter to shoot Hector as he did to kill Dom and Juno!'

Gloria wished Don wasn't home. The urge to scream her frustration at the top of her lungs was overwhelming. Seeking her last thread of control, she uttered a profanity.

'That man couldn't have been any more stupid if he had been trying.'

Tony meekly wondered, 'So the planting of the guns is out . . . right? I mean, now the cops know both shootings were done by the same person.'

'Put the weapons and stuff from Juno and Dom's place somewhere safe for the time being. If things get any worse, we might need them as evidence.'

'Evidence?' Tony gasped. 'Against whom?'

Gloria's mind was working, turning over ideas. 'I don't know yet. Just do as I tell you. Keep them someplace where you can get your hands on them at a minute's notice.'

'Now the theory of a gang war is out,' Tony said. Then he offered up an idea. 'Hey!' he said, suddenly pleased with himself. 'Maybe we could implicate one of the other street gangs? What if one of them wanted the Lobos and Hard Corps to go to war?'

Gloria shook her head. 'Don't start trying to think,' she warned sternly. 'It isn't your strong suit.'

'Yeah, but . . . '

'Let everything cool down for now. The police brought the two gang leaders in and talked to them. They are currently cooperating in a truce. With the same gun being responsible for both shootings, they will undoubtedly start to look elsewhere.'

'That's why a third gang would work,' Tony insisted.

Gloria took a deep breath to maintain her calm. 'I said to let me handle this. If you wanted to do the thinking, you should have thought about covering that rotten, filthy, accessible vent you have above your office couch!'

The strength left Tony's voice. 'All right, Glory honey. I'll put everything in a safe place. But I'll keep them where I can get them whenever you want.'

Gloria told him goodnight and hung up the phone.

'Trouble at work, babe?' Don asked, walking into the kitchen.

'They found out the same gun was used to killed the bangers from both gangs. It seems as if someone is trying to start a gang war.'

'You're talking about the attack on the judge's son and his roommate, plus that gang member from the Lobos?'

'Yes.'

'I read the article and it sounds as if someone might have killed Dominick Westmoreland by mistake.'

'Either that, or Dominick and his friend were into blackmail or something.'

Don frowned. 'Blackmail?'

Gloria shrugged. 'Or something. Those two

138

had come into a lot of money lately and the police can't figure out where it came from. No telling what kind of game they were playing, but they obviously crossed someone who didn't like it.'

'Do the police have any leads at all?'

Gloria didn't often share information with Don, but it was common ground. Don worked for Questar, the natural gas supplier for the valley. He spent most of his time supervising telephone reps, and that meant interacting and conversing with customers and employees. These attacks were probably a hot topic around the office.

'It's all pretty vague right now,' Gloria replied after a moment or two. 'Someone shot at the *Sentinel* reporter and that could be linked to her visit to the judge's son. She went to see him the day he was killed. The police really haven't figured anything out yet.'

'I hope it doesn't keep you awake all night,' Don said. 'You can't hold yourself responsible for every criminal act that takes place. It's too much for any one person.'

The words were spoken sincerely, but Gloria was worried that Don might one day guess she was cheating on him. Their time together had grown more uncomfortable and strained lately. With Tony to respond to her needs, Gloria had not been responsive to

Don's advances and their love had waned to mere cohabitation. A convenient headache or worry about a pending case was often her excuse for not allowing him his husbandly prerogatives. They each led their own lives . . . and now this.

Guilt washed over her like a cold rain, imbuing her with regret over the deaths of three young men. She had not intended that anyone should get hurt over her affair. If she could get through this and win re-election, she would file for divorce and surrender however much of her worth the court decided. It would be far more preferable to give up material things than to end up behind bars.

11

Kari stayed at Dee's house after the bridal shower ended, to help clean up.

'You don't have to stick around,' Dee contended. 'I'm sure you have much better ways to expend your energy.' She winked salaciously.

'You're hopeless, you know that?'

Dee feigned disappointment.

'I'm worried about you, kiddo,' she said. 'You should have held out for a guy who resides on our continent to fall in love with. Where's the fun in having a sweetheart if you remain celibate for the rest of your life?'

'We do have a major enigma in our relationship,' Kari admitted while helping to clear the table, 'Jason doesn't want to give up his job and neither do I. Unless someone invents a transporter that can zip one of us across the ocean in the blink of an eye, we're going to be spending eleven months of the year apart.'

'Can't he join the police force over here?'

'It's not just his job, Dee. His whole life is back in England.'

Dee picked up a remaining chocolate

donut from a pastry platter; it was giant size, nearly as big as a dinner plate. She wrapped it in a napkin and stuck it in the box she used to carry her lunch to work. At Kari's inquisitive look, she explained.

'I'm cutting back on sweets. My hubby has noticed that my love handles have handles of their own. He is also battling his own bulge, so we agreed to try and lose a few pounds. He is giving up fast-food lunches and I vowed to not have more than one pastry a day.'

'One five thousand calorie pastry,' Kari observed.

'Hey, I'm doing by best,' Dee was playfully defensive. 'It's like I told him last night. He promised to marry me for better or worse, so he shouldn't complain that he is getting more of me to enjoy every year.'

'And what did he say to that?'

Dee snorted. 'He said *'I married you for better, 'cause I didn't think you could get any worse!''*

Kari laughed at her jest. 'You're so bad!'

Dee exhibited a wide grin. 'So where is your sleuth boyfriend tonight?' she queried. Then quickly added, 'With whom you have yet to experience consummate bliss!'

'He is playing pool with Reggie and Tynan — Reggie's grandfather.'

'I would point out how you shouldn't share

what little time you have with the Brit, but seeing as how you aren't getting any loving, I don't suppose you are missing all that much.'

Kari sighed. 'Dee, you still have the dirtiest mind of anyone I know.'

Her friend grinned. 'You should get around more, kiddo; you'd see that I'm pretty normal.'

'If that's true, the population's moral compass is worse off than I ever imagined,' Kari retorted.

★ ★ ★

It was shortly before ten when Tynan announced he was ready to call it a night. Jason told Reggie he was going to drop in to see Kari, so the three of them parted company. He figured she would be home by this time and drove to her apartment. The two of them could discuss how their evenings had gone, then he would leave for Reggie's place with the taste of her sweet kiss on his lips.

Jason parked in the visitor's lot, got out, buttoned up his suit jacket and locked the rental car. As he approached Kari's building, he spotted a shadowy figure skulking in the shadows, near the entryway door. The security light wasn't very bright, but the man appeared to be dressed entirely in black and wearing a ski mask.

'Hold on!' Jason shouted, rushing to intercept the man, before he could flee for the sanctuary of the night.

The figure sprinted away, but wasn't exceptionally fast on his feet. Jason took a sharp angle and cut him off. 'Police!' he called out, moving to intercept him.

Instead of changing direction and trying to outrun Jason, the man suddenly veered and ran right at him. Jason slowed down and spread his arms, ready to block the man from getting past. Trying to stop a runaway truck on a steep hill would have been less of a chore.

The man lowered his shoulder and slammed flush against Jason's chest.

The force of the collision knocked Jason over backward. With his arms wrapped about the man, both men landed on the ground with the man on top of Jason. The wind was partially driven from his lungs but Jason recovered as the brute scrambled out of his grasp and tried to get to his feet. Reaching out, Jason managed to catch hold of the man's ankles with both hands and drag him back down.

Tackling an eel would have been easier. The guy was powerfully built and more than a match for Jason. He kicked and squirmed loose a second time, rose up as far as his knees and walloped Jason hard on the side of his head with a hammer-like fist. The blow stunned Jason and the tussle ended abruptly.

Groggy and helpless for several seconds, Jason managed to sit up. He was too late, as the shadowy figure had disappeared into the darkness. Gingerly rubbing the bruise near his temple, Jason took a moment to clear the fog from his brain and take a look around. As far as he could tell no cars had left the lot, so the man had not parked near the building. He groaned with frustration, having been thoroughly bested during the short exchange.

Bloody hell, Keane, he admonished himself. *Your attempt to nick that intruder ended in a total lash-up!*

★ ★ ★

Grady and Hampton were both red-eyed from being rousted from bed. There was no need to call the lab team as the man had been wearing gloves. Kari had fixed tea, which she and Jason were sipping while reclining on the loveseat together.

'So it was a fairly large guy and he ran you over?' Grady posed the question, but it sounded more like a critical evaluation.

Jason didn't conceal his angst. 'I must be getting past it. I had him in my grasp and let him get the better of me.'

'So that's all you can tell us?' Grady continued. 'You think the man was black, and he was a little bigger than your own height and weight. That's it?'

'That and he was built as solid as a bloody tank,' Jason added. 'Grabbing hold of him was like tackling a bull. He wasn't athletic, but seemed very fit, very muscular.'

'You said you thought he might be headed for Miss Underwood's apartment?' Hampton asked. 'What's your reasoning for that?'

'Because someone shot at her,' Jason replied.

'That could have only been a warning,' Grady concluded. 'Both shots were through the passenger side of the car.'

'That's true,' Jason said. 'But I believe that if you check the other residents in this building you won't find another likely target.'

'Do you think our killer meant to harm Miss Underwood tonight?' Hampton said.

'That much isn't clear, Detective. Someone might be afraid Dom and Juno gave Miss Underwood a piece of evidence or information. As you haven't determined how those two were earning so much extra money, we have no clue as to who is behind these attacks or what they are looking for.'

'Regardless, it's a good thing you stopped by,' Grady observed. 'A few minutes later — '

He didn't have to finish the sentence. As for Kari, she ignored the part about the sniper shooting at her and the intruder this evening. Instead, she was worried about Jason.

'You're lucky the prowler didn't severely hurt you.' Kari used a scolding tone of voice. 'What were you thinking?'

'He was thinking like a cop.' Hampton took up in his defense. 'It's just too bad he didn't get a look at the guy's face.'

'I wish I could have pulled off his ski-mask,' Jason informed them. 'If I had got a look at him . . . '

'He might have killed you!' Grady finished. 'That's something we don't need — a visiting cop ending up in the morgue during one of our investigations.'

'I too would have suffered a degree of humiliation if that happened,' Jason replied.

Hampton decided they were finished and directed his words at Kari. 'It's doubtful the man will return. However, we can post a patrol car to watch your place if you like?'

'No, that won't be necessary,' Kari replied.

'It's almost midnight,' Grady said. 'I don't think there's anything more to be learned from all of us losing more sleep.'

'Yeah, we're back on duty in a few hours,' Hampton complained. 'I don't know, Brit,' he directed his comment to Jason. 'Seems like every time you show up, we get run ragged for a couple weeks.'

'It's fortunate for you that I only visit occasionally.'

Grady laughed and patted Hampton on the arm. 'Let's get out of here. With a little luck we can get a few minutes of shuteye before the sun comes up.'

Kari let them out, locked the door behind them, and returned to sit down next to Jason. Concern shone brightly in her eyes. 'You might have been killed tonight.'

'The guy only wanted to get away.'

'Yes, but you didn't know that. You can't go around tackling possible killers with no weapon but your wits. These people are dangerous.'

'I won't argue that much, but I would bet money the prowler was on his way up to your apartment.'

Kari frowned. 'It makes no sense. I don't know anything.'

'Maybe you know something without realizing it. Or this guy might believe you can identify him. He might try again.'

'Thank you so much for your insight,' Kari

said drily. 'I'll sleep much better knowing a killer is stalking me.'

'Well, you've obviously done something to cause this character to be worried,' Jason said.

Kari leaned over and kissed him. When she pulled back, she tenderly murmured, 'Thank God you weren't hurt tonight. I don't know what I would do if anything happened to you.'

'I chose to intervene,' Jason replied. 'But I shall exercise more caution in the future.' He grinned. 'Like procuring a large club before a second encounter.'

Kari uttered a sigh. 'I've got to write this up and email the story to Scott.'

'While you do that I'm going to ring up Reggie. He's probably in bed by this time, but I need to let him know I won't be returning home tonight.'

Kari's expression was unreadable, but she leaned closer and murmured, 'That isn't necessary, Jason. Do you think you have to look after me?'

'You better flaming well believe it!'

At his staunch delivery, a coy smile lifted at the corners of her mouth. 'In that case, I'll sleep much better having you here.'

'I'll be fine on the couch,' he clarified quickly.

Her lips parted, as if she might object, but she didn't. With a slight tilt of her head, she said, 'All right.' Then she tenderly touched her lips to his. When she pulled back, a mysterious light danced within her eyes, and she added, ' . . . for tonight.'

★ ★ ★

The captain was not pleased. If his hard stare could have burned holes through solid objects, Grady and Hampton would have resembled used targets after a long day at the firing range.

'Did we misread the shooting at the reporter? Do we think this guy meant to kill her?'

'If he was armed, he didn't pull the weapon on the Brit,' Grady replied. 'We still don't know what his interest is in Miss Underwood.'

'We ran the other tenants in the building,' Ham put in. 'Most are poor working stiffs who barely get by from payday to payday. It's reasonable to assume the guy was headed for her apartment.'

'This gets better every day,' the captain lamented. 'The public is going to wonder why we weren't protecting the reporter.'

'A couple of warning shots don't add up to

a second attack, Capt'n,' Grady argued. 'We had no reason to think the shooter would actually go to her apartment. We figured it was possible that the shooting was only a ruse to cause us to focus in the wrong direction. And the prowler last night might have only been to throw an additional scare into Underwood.'

'Grady's got a point,' Hampton went along. 'The girl has told us again and again that she doesn't know anything. Maybe we're supposed to be chasing ghosts while the real case is something completely different. And there is an outside possibility that the guy last night was only a thief, looking to break into any one of the apartments.'

The captain was still scowling. 'We've got a hell of a case going. We know exactly nothing, so that makes every scenario a possibility.'

'At least we have a starting point on our perp,' Hampton said. 'We know his approximate height, weight, and he's built like a football linebacker.'

'Could be an ex-con,' Grady postulated. 'That's about all prisoners do while inside, work with weights and bulk up.'

'Add to the profile, the man we're looking for is an accomplished car thief,' the captain reminded them both. 'The first car had the

151

keys in it, but the one used during the killing of Hector Gomez was a hot-wire job.'

Grady scratched his head thoughtfully. 'Considering ballistics says the same gun was used to kill Juno and Hector, this doesn't appear to have anything to do with two gangs and a turf war. However, it might still be about the shipments of drugs coming in from Colombia.'

'The reporter claimed she got nothing from Dom and Juno,' Hampton reminded him. 'She put as much in the newspaper.'

The captain expressed his cynicism. 'If I'm linked to the cartel and receiving a priceless shipment every month, am I going to believe a reporter is telling the truth?'

'It's a thought,' Hampton agreed. 'We'll start looking at other angles on these attacks. Shooting a member of two different rival gangs could be a smoke screen, meant to keep us from looking in the right direction to stop those shipments.'

'Broaden your investigation to include any major drug connections,' the captain directed. 'Then pull the records of cons on the street, especially those who have stolen cars in the past and have a propensity for violence.'

'You got it, Capt'n,' Grady replied. 'We'll get on it right away.'

* ★ *

Kari was surprised at the phone call that came while she and Jason were having breakfast. It was from the district attorney's office, requesting she stop by first thing that morning.

'Probably about your nocturnal visitor, the one I allowed to escape,' Jason speculated, once she had hung up the receiver. 'I'd better go along with you and repeat my account of my humiliation in allowing him to get the better of me.'

Kari grinned. 'We could embellish it a little, say how the guy took you by surprise and attacked you from behind?'

'We Brits always accept proper due for our own cock-ups,' he stated smugly.

'I will have to spend some time at my desk today,' Kari advised him. 'It might be noon or later before I get out to the field for further interviews.'

'I'm sure I can find something to keep myself occupied. You can ring me up on my mobile when you're ready.'

'You mean it's actually working?'

Jason chuckled. 'I threatened to start filing for expenses from using pay phones, so the department gave me a new one the day I left. It's rather an improvement

153

— takes photographs and I can receive information and photos of a suspect. Unlike me, it's very modern and up to date.'

A short while later, Jason accompanied Kari to the DA's office. A pleasant secretary with a name plate 'Dotty' greeted them. She punched an intercom button and a woman's voice answered.

'Kari Underwood and a gentleman from the *Sentinel* are here to see you.'

'Thank you. I'll be with her in minute,' came the reply.

Dotty said OK and smiled up at Kari.

'I've got a daughter who would love to see her team mentioned in the Sports section. She and her teammates are undefeated so far this year.' She laughed. 'Of course, the season has just begun, so we're only talking about three games, but she is very excited.'

Kari said she knew a couple of the staff writers and, if Dotty emailed her the information, she would mention the team to one of them. Before the secretary could thank her, the door opened. A handsome fellow appeared and held the door for them to enter.

'Tony Martin,' he introduced himself. 'I'm one of Mrs. Streisand's deputy district attorneys. We have both been following the gang related shootings that have taken place in the last few days.'

Once the man had closed the door behind them Kari introduced Jason to Gloria and the DDA.

'I remember your deposition during the Coin Killer case last year,' Gloria said in greeting Jason. 'I've no doubt you are a credit to the Sutton CID.'

'I've done my best to make them believe I am indispensable,' Jason replied.

Gloria motioned to Tony, who handed her a sheet of paper. Jason observed that they were very comfortable standing close while examining the document. Their shoulders rubbed as Tony pointed out a section for Gloria's attention.

'You tackled a prowler outside Miss Underwood's apartment last night?' Gloria inquired.

Jason knew how the report read, but explained the details of the short encounter. 'He was at least thirty pounds heavier than me and very fit,' he finished. 'If he had a car near by, I didn't see it.'

Gloria eyed Kari with a glowing suspicion. 'When we last spoke, you said you had gotten no information from Dom and Juno. Why should this man come after you?' She added a second question, 'Is it possible you know something but don't realize what it is?'

'I can only assume this is the guy who was

watching Juno and Dom's place. He must think I got a good look at his face, but I didn't.'

'And you are not working on anything else that might be explosive in some way?'

'No, ma'am,' Kari replied. 'I've gone over every story I've done in the past few months — the detectives have, too — and there isn't anything.'

'The killer was looking for something at Juno's house. He took their phones and computer. During your interview, did you inquire about anything that might have been related to information that might be stored on one of those devices?'

'Nothing whatsoever,' Kari responded. 'The two young men pretty much ran me off without telling me anything.'

'It makes no sense why someone is after you.' Tony spoke up. 'I mean, if you didn't get any information, and Dom and Juno didn't give you anything of value, then why would this guy come after you?'

Before Kari could answer the DA changed the subject. 'I was told you were interviewing people about these murders?'

'Only as a follow-up to the police briefings,' Kari told her. 'I haven't spoken to or visited any gang members.'

'Yes, I don't think that would be wise. The

Hard Corps might hold you responsible for getting Juno killed.'

'Same goes for the 39th Street Lobos and Hector's death,' Tony interjected. 'Could have been a member of either of those gangs who was prowling around at your apartment last night.'

'I've assured the detectives that I will share anything I find with them immediately,' Kari promised the DA.

'Do you wish to request police protection?' Gloria asked. 'I can call the chief.'

'No, Jason is going to stick close to me until this is settled.'

'How very . . . ' Gloria searched for the right word and Tony finished it with, ' . . . Gallant.'

Jason grinned. 'That's a title I didn't exactly earn last night.'

'You ran him off.' Gloria commended his actions. 'It would have been more beneficial had you captured him, but Miss Underwood is safe. That is the first priority.'

'It certainly is,' Jason agreed.

'Thank you for stopping by.' Gloria bid farewell to them. 'If you should suddenly think of something that could help, my door is always open.'

Outside the office Dotty greeted them with a professional smile again. 'Was Mrs.

Streisand able to help you?'

'It was interesting,' Kari replied. 'Is she a good boss?'

Dotty flicked a glance at the door, making sure it was closed. 'She's . . . ' looking for the right word, 'a challenge to work for,' was her answer. 'She's very demanding, which is the very opposite of her husband. He's one of those easy going sorts, always in a good mood, with nothing bad to say about anyone or anything. They seem an odd coupling.'

'Does he come here often?'

'Not nearly as much as he used to. He used to visit almost daily, but now it's only occasionally to have lunch together or something.'

'It was nice meeting you,' Kari said. 'Send me that email and I'll call you after I speak to my friend in the sporting news.'

'Thank you,' Dotty said. 'My daughter would be thrilled.'

As Jason and Kari left the building, Kari expelled a deep breath. 'That DA is a formidable woman, I felt like I was the suspect in the shootings.'

'Her aide positively hung on her every word,' Jason replied. 'And did you notice how they seemed to finish each other's sentences?'

Kari gave him an inquisitive look. 'You don't think there's some hanky-panky going on between Gloria and her DDA?'

'I was merely making an observation.'

Kari's brow furrowed in thought. 'If they are more than working together, it would be something of a scandal. Gloria is up for re-election and Tony was wearing a wedding ring.'

'Perhaps I misread their relationship,' Jason said. Then, moving forward, 'What now?'

'I have to go in and do a follow-up on your encounter last night. As this is all first-hand reporting, Scott intends to enjoy the scoop.'

'I'll pop over to see the detectives and compare notes. Maybe I can pick up a bit of fodder for your next article. I'll have my mobile turned on. Let me know when you are ready to leave.'

'This shouldn't take long,' Kari said. Then she looped her arm inside his and they started walking back to the *Sentinel* building.

12

Gloria fumed inwardly as she walked down the corridor. Lincoln had made another blunder, thinking the reporter was not at home and nearly being caught by the Brit. Tony excused the mistake by saying Lincoln had seen that the Englishman's rental car was not in the visitors' lot and he figured the two of them were out on the town. It was a plausible assumption, but one that could have been catastrophic. If Underwood knew anything or had any information, she would be doubly on the alert now.

The notion stuck in Gloria's head: Kari must know something. She had been snooping around Juno's family members. She had also talked to the Westmorelands. Gloria worried that Dom might have said something to cause Kari suspicion about her and Tony's affair.

Suddenly her thought process came to a halt. Paul Hanson was striding down the hallway. The man smiled a greeting — a hungry weasel pausing to scrutinize a lone chicken in the henhouse.

'Gloria! How nice to see you.' He stuck out

his hand. 'How's the re-election campaign going?'

Hating to make physical contact with her opponent, she nevertheless succumbed to shake his hand briefly. 'I've other things to worry about at the moment, Paul. You know we're facing a crisis with these gang shootings.'

'Don't forget the reporter,' he remarked. 'I understand someone tried to get into her apartment last night?' He shook his head. 'Makes one wonder what she knows.'

'I spoke to her only moments ago and she claims to not have a clue as to why anyone would be after her.'

'Evidently the killer believes she knows something,' Paul opined. 'Do you think she learned something important from Juno or Dom and simply doesn't know what it means?'

An icy shard lodged in Gloria's chest. She hid the feeling and tried to not appear interested. 'What could Dom have told her? He wasn't a gang member.'

'Perhaps it has nothing to do with gangs,' Paul suggested. 'He worked in this building. He may have overheard a private conversation or found a piece of sensitive material in the trash.'

Gloria countered, 'I don't think Dom

would have risked getting fired over eaves-dropping or snooping in the trash,'

'There are some odd things happening lately,' Paul changed the direction of their conversation. 'Like a weapons charge being dropped on a repeat offender a few days back. That was courtesy of one of your DDAs.'

'If you are talking about Chock Lincoln, I approved his action. The man explained he was afraid for his life. That's why he was carrying a gun when he was picked up. I didn't want the media to jump on the idea that we were singling him out for prosecution because he was black.'

'You're right,' Paul allowed. 'The media lives to promote divisive issues, and this town has a great many people who are radically sensitive when race is involved.'

'I don't see why it's any concern of yours. If I recall, you were recently targeted by a Hispanic organization for recommending deportation for undocumented workers who were caught with small amounts of cocaine.'

'Yes, we live in trying times,' Paul conceded, again with a professional smile. 'And I'm sure you are under extreme pressure to find Dom's killer because of who his father is.'

'Speaking of Judge Westmoreland, the man is waiting for me.'

'Of course. Don't let me keep you, Gloria.' A glimmer of complacency shone in his eyes. 'I know you're a very busy woman.' He added: 'It's a wonder you and your husband find any time at all to be together.'

Gloria suffered a twinge of guilt at his bringing up that subject, but replied nonchalantly. 'I try and keep my home life separate from my work.'

'It's wonderful that you and I both have such strong marriages.' He made it a statement. Then he stepped around her and walked on down the hall.

Gloria set her teeth firmly together to control the bile which rose up from deep inside of her. She was fearful now. Tony had been worried that Paul knew about their relationship. After this repartee with him, she also was concerned.

Does the man actually know something, or is he merely testing the waters, searching for a reaction?

★ ★ ★

The meeting with Grady and Hampton resulted in more than Jason had expected. Grady had him look over the official incident

163

report about his confrontation with the suspected prowler, then handed him over to Hampton. The senior detective opened a desk drawer, removed a gun and shoulder holster, then handed the weapon to Jason.

'Here you go — a six-inch, .357 Magnum revolver. Only six shots, but it has the stopping power to do the job. The weather is about right for you to wear a suit jacket. That should hide the bulge of being armed.'

Jason accepted the gun, removed it and felt the familiar weight and balance. 'It's been a while, but I have actually fired one of these a number of times,' he told them. 'As you know, back in the CID, we seldom carry a weapon unless we expect armed resistance.'

'You have the reporter to protect.' Hampton supported the decision to allow him to carry a weapon. 'Shots through her windshield, a second episode last night . . . we don't know what this guy wants.'

'That,' Grady said, 'is why the captain gave permission for you to carry a gun. He even rounded up a special gun permit for you.' Grady produced a small slip of paper and passed it to Jason.

'Do us a favor and don't shoot anyone,' Hampton joked. 'The paperwork for something like that would be unbelievable.'

Jason grinned, 'I shall try and control the

impulse when it comes to rude drivers and children throwing tantrums in public.'

'This perp might believe you happened to be there by accident last night, or he could know you are watching Miss Underwood. Either way, he is going to be more careful. Keep your eyes open.'

Hampton handed him a box of ammunition. 'If you need more than this, you'll have to buy the bullets yourself. We don't keep a lot of extra ammo around the office.'

'If I can't hit a specified target with an entire box of shells, I would be better off throwing rocks.'

★ ★ ★

'I don't know, Kari,' Dee was saying during their coffee break, 'You said the Brit is staying with you . . . but he sleeps on the couch?' She made a face, as if she had a bitter taste in her mouth. 'You sure your boyfriend was ever married? Doesn't he know the rules for wooing a girl?'

'It's complicated,' Kari replied. 'You know the terrible experience I had with Roger, and his one and only relationship was with his wife.'

'But this is the twenty-first century, kiddo. Don't you watch television? If you haven't slept with your fella by the third date, one or both of you must be gay!'

'I worry about you sometimes, Dee. Is this the same talk you gave to your kids concerning sex?'

'More or less.' Dee grinned. 'Except I told them that, if they had sex before they were twenty-one, life as they knew it would come to an immediate end.'

'I thought so.'

'Yes, but they weren't over the hill like you.'

'Over the hill? I'll be twenty-seven on my next birthday.'

'OK, so you're teetering on the precipice of the mountain crest. The point is, you're running out of time.'

Kari brought up the obituary on Juno Orozco and studied the page.

'You thinking of getting back into obits?' Dee asked. 'I thought you'd seen enough of those to last a lifetime.'

'I have. But I wonder if we overlooked a clue about these murders.'

'What's your thinking, kiddo?'

'I don't know,' she complained to Dee. 'We're missing something.'

'I told you, don't let the Brit sleep on the couch. Get him in bed with you and let nature take its course.'

Kari exhaled a sigh of exasperation and

patiently said, 'I was referring to the murder victims.'

'Um, I thought we were talking about something of real importance.'

Kari's phone rang and she paused to answer it. 'Oh, hi!' she greeted the caller. It was Dotty from the DA's office. 'Yes, I got the information you emailed me. Do you think you can help with my reply?'

Dotty answered that she could and gave Kari the information.

'Of course. I don't want you to get into trouble over this.' Another pause to listen, then Kari flashed a smile at Dee and finished the call. 'What time will that be?' After a short pause she replied, 'Thank you so much, and I'll make sure we get that article printed about your daughter's soccer team.'

'What's up?' Dee asked, as soon as Kari returned the phone to its cradle.

'Gloria Streisand's secretary sent me an email for Jerry, over in sports.'

'Yeah, Jerry's a softie. If he was my man, I'd have him on a diet.' She laughed. 'Well, maybe not. If there was only one pastry left in the house, I might need an edge to beat him to it!'

'Anyway,' Kari continued with her story. 'I mentioned to Dotty how I'd like to get a look at Gloria's husband. She said he used to visit

Gloria at her office all the time, but he seldom comes by now. Anyhow, Dotty said Don called a little while ago and wanted to make sure Gloria's calendar was clear. He'd made a reservation for them tonight over at Flemming's Steak House.'

'So you're going to be there at the same time so you can spy on her?'

'It's not spying; it's complicated. I'm curious is all.'

A look of sisterly concern flooded Dee's features. 'You be careful, kiddo,' she warned. 'You remember what happened the last time you and the Brit got mixed up with a case? You might have been resting quietly in a box, six feet under ground, if the cops hadn't sent someone in your place to meet with that psycho at the motel.'

'It's a night out on the town, not an investigation.'

'Don't con me, kiddo,' Dee said. 'I can read you like a book. You are sticking your nose deeper into these gang killings and Gloria is not going to like it.'

'I'll be fine. Jason will be with me.'

'Yes, but he proved last night that he wasn't James Bond,' Dee reminded her. 'And you can count your blessings for that . . . considering all of the women James Bond has gotten killed!'

Judge Westmoreland greeted Gloria with a forced smile when she entered his chambers. She took a chair opposite his desk and waited for him to say what was on his mind.

'I saw ballistics matched the gun to both my son's and Hector Gomez's murders. Where does that leave us on a motive for the shootings?'

'It's unknown at this point,' Gloria answered. 'We think this might have something to do with drugs being shipped in from Colombia and the *Sentinel* reporter, Kari Underwood. Unfortunately, she swears ignorance on the matter.'

'Dom and Juno had a lot of money from doing something. What have you uncovered about that?'

'A friend of Juno's said they were doing some odd jobs on the side, but he didn't know what kind of work or for whom. It's also possible they saw or knew something and used it to coerce payment from someone. It could be what got them killed.'

'You mean blackmail?'

'We have no way of knowing. But their cellular phones, iPads and computers were taken; plus the killer made a thorough search of the house. The police found no pictures or cameras, no stash of money or goods, nothing to give us any idea as to what the killer might have been looking for.'

The judge pounded a fist on the top of his desk. 'Damn it all, Gloria!' he cried, his face contorted by his pain and helpless frustration. 'Someone killed my son. I want to know why this happened.'

Gloria suffered her own degree of misery. 'I'm sorry, Your Honor,' she murmured. 'I wish I had an answer for you.'

Westmoreland recouped his composure, regaining his usual temperate disposition. 'I didn't mean to raise my voice.'

'It's perfectly understandable, Judge.'

The judge set aside his personal tragedy for a moment. 'I heard that Paul Hanson has received the endorsement of the Teachers Union. That could hurt you in the upcoming election.'

'He's playing the same game as all politicians,' Gloria responded. 'Say what the people want to hear and they will vote for you.'

'He has been successful as a prosecuting attorney. You are going to have your hands full with this fight.' When she did not reply the judge leaned over the desk and spoke in a no-nonsense manner. 'I brought up the election because you need a big win to solidify the support you need to defeat Hanson. Finding the killer of my son would go a long way when it comes to getting those votes.'

'I'm aware of that,' Gloria said.

Westmoreland tipped his head forward slightly, acknowledging the meeting had ended. 'Thank you for sharing your time, Ms District Attorney.'

Gloria rose to her feet. 'Any time, Your Honor,' she reciprocated. Then she pivoted about and left the room.

★ ★ ★

As Kari was making the drive to the Flemming's Steak House, Jason queried about their intentions. 'Tell me again, why are we interested in the district attorney's marriage?'

'It's hard to put into words,' Kari answered. 'You know how you occasionally get a vibe off of someone, that everything isn't as it seems?' At his gesture of comprehension, she went on. 'Well, I'm getting that vibe from Gloria Streisand and don't know why.'

'Explain if you would.'

'It's the way she has come at me in our interviews. It's like she thinks I'm holding something back, something important. She asks questions that are pointed and direct, but not exactly on target with the investigation.'

'What possible information could you be holding back?'

'I'm not sure.'

'She might be overly sensitive, if she is having an affair.'

Kari frowned. 'Until you mentioned the way she and her DDA interacted, I didn't suspect anything like that.'

'What kind of questions did she ask you on your previous meeting, to make you wary of her motives?'

'She made repeated attempts to solicit a reaction or response to my being involved in a vague project or secret investigation of some kind. You saw how she was today, acting as if I was hiding something from her. She makes me feel more like a suspected perpetrator than a witness or reporter.'

Jason considered her deductions before he inquired, 'So what are we hoping to learn from this evening's mission?'

Kari laughed without humor. 'Honestly, I haven't a clue.'

'Unfortunately, logic dictates that lacking an actual goal significantly increases the likelihood of failure,' Jason prophesied. Then he added with a grin, 'Perhaps the food will be compensation if we come away having learned nothing.'

She displayed an impish simper. 'You have a delightful way of saying you think I'm wasting my time, but you're willing to go along with my quest.'

'You might prefer to think of it more as my endorsement of your intuition as a reporter.'

'I must say, I was surprised the detectives provided you with a gun.'

'Thankfully, they were not privy to my scores from the shooting range.'

Kari threw him an *are-you-kidding?* look, and Jason laughed.

★ ★ ★

The phone rang after Grady had barely sat down to dinner with his wife and three kids. Regardless of his hours or the stress of a case, he always tried to be there for supper with the family.

His wife was at the stove and closest to the phone. She answered and several lines furrowed her brow. 'Deroy Hampton.' Her voice held a scolding tone. 'You know we eat promptly at six 'o clock every night.'

Hampton must have apologized because Leta's expression softened. She uttered a sigh of resignation and asked, 'How soon?'

Another moment.

'I'll tell him.' A short pause, then she said, 'Yes, I understand. Goodbye.'

'What did Ham want?' Grady asked, as soon as she had hung up the receiver.

'There's been another shooting, over at Liberty Park. No one is seriously hurt, but Deroy wants you to meet him there as soon as you can.'

Grady started to get up, but his wife's sharp look stopped him in mid-motion. 'He said you could take time to eat,' she directed firmly. 'I didn't fix fried chicken so you would up and run out without eating. You do realize it is something of a feat to prepare a big meal with three kids underfoot?'

'I sure do, Kitten,' Grady praised. 'You're a combination mother, magician and angel all rolled into one.'

The flattery removed the stern look from her face. 'Fifteen minutes,' she negotiated. 'You can give us that much of your time.'

Grady smiled appreciatively. 'That won't be long enough for me tonight. I always eat more than I should when you fix chicken.'

Leta joined them at the table and Grady took a moment to say grace. Once everyone was filling their plates, his wife commented, 'I thought you told me the gangs had vowed to keep the peace?'

'Actually, the only thing we did was convince two of the valley's gang leaders that neither side was responsible for the recent killings.' He took a big bite of chicken breast, chewed a moment, then asked, 'Did Ham say which gangs were involved?'

'No.' Leta blushed slightly. 'I didn't give him a lot of time for explanation.'

'My kitten,' Grady chuckled affectionately. 'My little wildcat!'

13

The steak house was set up with corner booths, but most customers were seated at tables and chairs. With numerous partitions, live plants and hanging vines, the garden decor made it difficult to see many of the other patrons. As the hostess led them though the dining area Kari spotted the DA and her husband among the lavishly dressed guests.

'This would be perfect.' She stopped the hostess next to a table for two. 'It's both private and secluded.'

The girl looked as if she would refuse, but Jason reached out and tucked a twenty-dollar bill into her hand. 'We would be most appreciative,' he said, using an enticing smile that caused Kari's eyebrows to raise.

The girl glimpsed the denomination of the bill and immediately returned Jason's smile. 'Of course,' she agreed courteously. 'Let me exchange the number from the table and replace it with your reservation.'

'Jolly good,' Jason said. 'You're most charming and obliging.' The girl hurried to switch the small triangular placard which displayed a number on either side. Jason removed Kari's coat and draped it over the back of her chair. By the time they were both seated, the hostess had completed the task.

Kari purposely looked down at her shoes, then shot him a snide look. 'I hope the stuff you were shoveling to that girl doesn't stick to my new shoes.'

Before Jason could respond, Kari glanced Gloria's direction. The simper froze on her lips. Gloria had spotted her and was studying her with a hateful glare.

'Uh-oh, we've been seen,' she murmured to Jason.

'That didn't take long.'

Kari figured it was better to acknowledge Gloria than ignore her. She forced a smile of recognition and raised a hand to wave at her. Her husband was average looking, with a few extra pounds and thinning hair. She could not discern much from a single glance, but he looked tired and . . . *beaten down* was the notion that came to mind. He reminded her of someone who had been reprimanded and had accepted his fate. Gloria acknowledged her wave with a simple nod of her head and Kari purposely turned away, as if completely absorbed in her own conversation with Jason.

'That woman must have eyes like an eagle. We didn't even get seated before she saw us.'

Jason didn't look in their direction, but

stated, 'In the investigative field one learns that a guilty person is always more observant than an innocent one.' He smiled, as if they were discussing some trifle. 'Why should the DA be concerned about you seeing her with her husband?'

Kari forced a laugh, as if Jason had said something funny. 'I have no idea.'

'Will her knowing you are here change what you hoped to learn?'

Kari shook her head. 'I'm not sure. I wanted to see how Gloria behaved, how she interacted with her husband.'

'Because we suspect that she and one of her DDAs is having an affair?'

'You're the one who pointed it out to me — the touching, how comfortable they were while working side by side. They seemed more than co-workers.'

'Ignore the DA for now,' Jason advised, carefully adjusting his suit jacket to hide the bulge of his concealed weapon. He picked up a menu and proposed, 'Let's order and behave normally. If we are discreet, we might yet observe if the two of them are getting on.'

Kari put her attention on the list of entrées. It was a complicated situation, and she had no idea what Gloria could possibly have to do with anything. Even if she were having a fling with her DDA, what did that prove? What possible connection could her personal indiscretion have to do with the way she had interrogated Kari? Was her intensity due to her eagerness to solve the death of Judge Westmoreland's son, or did the woman think Kari knew something that could be detrimental to her personally?

★ ★ ★

The two Lobo gang members were not seriously injured, but both of them were unnerved by their encounter. The paramedics were on the scene and one Lobo had a bandage wrapped about the calf of his leg. The boys' street names were Neon and Gabrio.

'So how did this come to a shooting?' Grady asked the pair. 'What were you two up to?'

'We was looking for the guy who wasted Hector,' Neon replied. 'Word around the 'hood was there were a couple of Brazilian dudes doing some big time dealing 'round town. We figured something heavy was going down and come for a look.'

'True that,' Gabrio confirmed. 'We showed up and them dudes began to bust caps at us!'

'Gabe and me booked,' Neon said. 'But they hit him in the leg, so I stopped to help him. Them thug-nasty dudes kept tossing bullets so we made like a couple of groundhogs and burrowed for cover.'

'How bad are you injured?' Grady asked the wounded man.

'Bled some, but I been hit worse.'

'You two never saw these guys before?'

Neon answered, 'Sum Nervous Nellies they was, banging away at us afore we even got close. They was *fo' sho'* into something *sketchy.*'

'Could have been the monthly drug shipment from the Colombian cartel?' Grady suggested.

'Another witness saw two dark colored SUVs parked on the circle drive,' a uniform, who had been first on the scene, told Grady. 'Both vehicles were gone by the time the gunfire died down.'

Hampton grunted. 'It plays out these two Lobos happened along about the time the transaction was taking place and those characters got spooked.'

'How many shots were fired?' Grady asked the pair.

'More than Gabe and me could count!' Neon replied.

'All right,' Hampton told the uniform. 'We've got all we're going to get from these two. Have them transported to the hospital.

Then see if there are any surveillance cameras in the area.'

'It's already being checked out,' the cop replied.

Hampton waited until the two Lobos were taken away by ambulance before patting Grady on the shoulder.

'Sorry about calling you out on this. I could have handled it alone.'

'You didn't have any information. This was a shooting — a drug deal gone wrong, an escalation of a gang war or worse — you couldn't have known.'

'I have to wonder if it was the cartel,' Hampton said. 'This is pretty public for an exchange.'

'It's possible they think it was necessary. Underwood may have them running scared.'

'You and I know she hasn't found anything concrete.'

'That isn't the point, Ham. They only have to believe she knows something. It would have been enough to have them change their normal delivery.'

'Ke-ripes, Grady!' Ham declared. 'If they start thinking our star reporter actually *does* know something ... ' He didn't have to finish.

'We ought to alert the Brit,' said Grady. 'If anything hinky should happen, he would be able to deal with it.' He thought about it for a moment. 'Maybe we ought to put a team to watch them.'

Hampton did not agree. 'If we did that, it would be like confirming the suspicion that Underwood does know something. It would invite some kind of attack.'

'I'm beginning to wonder if the sniper who shot at Miss Underwood intended it as a warning, or did the sun's reflection off of her windshield ruin his aim?' Grady didn't wait for an answer, but continued. 'And what if the prowler went to her apartment intending to kill her?'

'Only one prowler and only one shooter?' Hampton posed the question. 'That doesn't have the marks of a hit squad from a drug cartel.' He heaved a sigh. 'No, I think there's something else going on.'

'Yeah, but what?'

'No idea,' Hampton admitted. Then back to Kari, 'You got the Brit's cell number?'

'He calls it a mo-bile,' Grady drawled. 'But, yeah, I'll give him a heads-up about this.'

'Right. We'll check with the captain tomorrow and get his thoughts on how he wants to proceed.'

* * *

Jason had begun another challenging night of sleeping on Kari's sofa, but the phone rang as he was trying to find a comfortable position.

Kari picked up the extension in her bedroom but he couldn't make out what was said. A moment later, the kitchen light switched on and Kari entered the room.

Jason stared, agog at the sight. Kari was clad in a short, pink-with-white-lace negligée. With the light behind her, the outfit was mildly translucent, revealing the feminine contours of her body. She didn't appear to notice his being dumbstruck as she glided across the room, to stop in front of him.

'It's for you,' she informed him, unable to hide her curiosity. 'It's Detective Grady.'

Jason sat up and, summoning an extraordinary amount of self control, managed enough chivalry to raise his gaze to look Kari in the face. 'He's calling me?'

'He said he tried your cell but it was not turned on.'

Jason rose to his feet, feeling quite exposed himself, clad in only a T-shirt and boxers. He moved quickly over to pick up the living room receiver. 'This is Jason Keane.'

He listened intently to Grady and said only a word or two in reply. Then he replaced the unit on the telephone set. He glanced at Kari, once again unable to prevent his eyes from lingering on the inviting lingerie and her shapely bare legs. Instead of embarrassment, she gave him an impatient look, raised expectant eyebrows and asked, 'Well?'

'Uh, there was a shooting at a place called Liberty Park. Grady thought it might be an interrupted drug deal. A couple of the 39th Street Lobos showed up and were driven off by gunfire. One of the Lobos was injured, but it was only a slight leg wound.'

'Why call you?'

'He thought I might be more forthcoming than you about anything you had learned about the cartel.'

Kari displayed a tight little frown. 'The detectives think you would tell them something I wouldn't?' She scrutinized him for a long moment, undoubtedly thinking he had not told her everything. 'Why would you do that?'

'Professional courtesy, I suppose.'

'What else did he say?'

'Only that I should continue to look after you.' Jason granted her a portion of the truth.

Kari was unconvinced but let the matter drop. 'Scott will be upset if I don't try and get the information on the shooting tonight.'

'Grady said there would be no formal statement until the morning briefing. You couldn't put much of a story together if you tried.'

Kari crossed her arms, as if suddenly aware of her skimpy outfit. However, the next words she spoke were critical in a way Jason was not expecting.

'You can't keep trying to sleep on that loveseat. I don't know how you manage to get any rest at all.'

Jason swallowed against a rise of desire. It was impossible to ignore the physical attraction he felt or dismiss the radiance of Kari's beauty, especially when she was decorated like a model for a men's magazine. When she stepped over next to him, he detected the scent of her perfume and was overcome by her nearness. He reached out and corralled her in his arms.

'You know, every man has his breaking point.' The words came out husky and impassioned. 'Being this close is not a wise decision, not with you dressed as you are.'

Kari teased his lips with a fleeting kiss and an impish mischievousness danced in her eyes. 'Don't tell me your English cast-iron will is weakening?'

'Melted like my heart whenever I'm around you.'

She matched his desire with a cool sincerity. 'We might live worlds apart, Jason, but I want us to be together.' Her voice softened to a gentle murmur. 'I want to share my love with you. If we only have each other for a few weeks a year, I'm willing to settle for that.'

'I don't know if I can,' he replied candidly. 'If I make love to you, I will want you by my side for ever.'

Rather than continuing an irresoluble debate, Kari retreated a step from his embrace and turned toward the bedroom. Taking his hand in her own, she gave a slight tug. Jason was helpless to do anything but follow.

When the morning light first peeked through the bedroom curtains, Kari was still lying in his arms. Jason was awake long before she stirred but waited until she opened her eyes to change positions.

'I've got to get to work,' she whispered, rising playfully up to nip his ear. 'That story from last night will have to be written. I'll also have to attend the briefing from the chief of police.'

'I'll drop you at work and visit our favorite detectives. Maybe I can pick up something extra for you to add to your article.'

'That's very thoughtful of you, Jason. I only wish we didn't spend so much of our time together chasing stories.'

'It can't be helped,' he said.

Kari rose up onto her elbows and kissed him. 'I wish you could stay here with me.'

Jason pulled her to him and held her tightly in his arms. 'And I wish I could take you home with me.'

Kari hesitated before she inquired: 'Could you possibly stay? I mean, if we were to get married, you would be eligible for citizenship in two years. You could start a new life over here.'

'I have a job to do back home,' he countered. 'I worked hard to make detective inspector and am in line for chief inspector. It's a job I'm good at.'

'Would you have to start over here?' she asked. 'You've proved your worth to the local detectives. Maybe you wouldn't have to wait very long to move up in our law enforcement.'

'There is always a chain of organization in place. I might be given some benefit for my experience, but there would be a lot of men ahead of me for any future promotions. I have no desire to return to being a uniform police officer again.'

Kari pursed her lips in thought. 'I could give up my job and go with you?'

Jason smiled. 'I know how hard you've worked to get where you are now. Not knowing how anything works in my country, and being an American, you would be lucky to land a position posting death notices with one of our news agencies.'

He ducked his head, filled with desire, yet conflicted by the hopelessness of their relationship. 'I knew I shouldn't have taken this step. Leaving you is going to be the hardest thing I've ever done in my life.'

'Love will find a way, Jason,' Kari said softly. 'Somehow, we'll make this work.'

'Take your shower and get ready for work,' Jason said. 'I'll put on tea and prepare some eggs, ham and waffles for breakfast.'

Kari kissed him and cast him a longing look. 'About the time I have you broke in to cater to my every whim, you'll up and go back to England. Life can be very cruel sometimes.'

14

Dee walked by Kari's cubicle to say good morning. Even before Kari managed a greeting, the woman swooped in and stood over her, scrutinizing her with a hawkish stare. 'Do I see . . . ?' She eyed Kari as if studying a lab slide under a microscope. 'Did you and the Brit . . . ?' A closer, more intense peruse brought a flush to Kari's cheeks — 'You did!' she cried.

'Dee!' Kari scolded her. 'For heaven's sake!'

But Dee was as gleeful as if she had just won the lottery. 'Hallelujah!' she cheered. 'It's about time.' Then she leaned over and hugged Kari. 'I was so worried that you and Jason, that the two of you . . . that he would break your heart.'

'Goodness, Dee!' Kari sputtered. 'You've totally lost your mind!'

Dee let go of her but continued to hover. 'So?' she asked.

'So what?'

'You know what!' she insisted. 'Are you compatible? Did you feel the earth move? Bells ring? Birds sing?'

'Did you ever suffer from vertigo or tinnitus from making love to your husband?' Kari retorted bluntly.

Dee simmered a few degrees. 'No, but one time a cop with a flashlight did cause my heart to about leap out of my chest!'

'You're hopeless.'

'OK, OK,' she giggled. 'I'm just happy you finally got him to commit. I was beginning to worry.' She shook her head. 'You know, loving someone you only see a few weeks a year is hard enough. But to not enjoy each other fully during the actual time you have . . . well, it's . . . it's unhealthy, both physically and for your morale.'

'I'm sure there are psychiatrists who agree with you.' Kari smirked. 'And I'm equally sure they would have a great time studying your brain. Its unique workings are like nothing I've ever heard of before.'

Dee grinned, 'You mean because of my sharp wit and keen insight when it comes to personal relations?'

'That's a nice way of saying you're nosy and dirty-minded.'

Their teasing came to an abrupt end when a young lad, Tommy, from the mailroom, approached and stopped at Kari's work station.

'Here's something strange for you, Miss

Underwood,' he said. 'Maybe you've got an admirer?'

Kari accepted an envelope with only her name scribbled on the outside. Tommy left, but Dee stood and waited for her to open the unusual piece of mail. Inside was an anonymous note. There was no return address and no signature. She quickly read it aloud.

Miss Underwood:
Everyone has assumed that Dom and Juno were killed because of something to do with drugs. I suggest you consider this might have been about blackmail and one of our DDAs.
A concerned citizen.

'Here we go again!' Dee was breathless. 'What is it about you, kiddo? Do you have to attract every nut in the valley?'

Kari reread it a second time and felt gooseflesh rise along her arms and down her back. Her stomach roiled with an inner rush of nerves and she discovered her hands were trembling.

'I've got to speak to Scott,' she told Dee.

'I'll catch up with you later,' Dee said. 'Don't you get into anything that will get you shot at again!'

As Dee left the cubicle Kari picked up her phone and punched the button for the editor's office. He came on the line a few seconds later and she explained about the anonymous letter.

'What's your take on this?' Scott asked.

'It would support a feeling I've had.' Kari told him about Gloria's aggressive interrogations. 'And it would explain why she was so concerned that Dom and Juno might have told me or given me something.'

'You think Gloria might know about the blackmail?'

'It's possible. Her office might be quietly looking into something that we know nothing about.'

'But the note clearly states one of the deputy district attorneys was involved. It doesn't mention her personally, does it?'

'No. It's exactly as I read it to you,' Kari concurred. 'However, it does fit the missing electronic gadgets and search of the boys' house. It's possible someone learned about the blackmail and wanted to acquire the material and use it for a reason of their own.'

'That's possible. Talk to Jason and see what he thinks,' Scott suggested. 'We can't do much with a single piece of unsubstantiated information, but he might have an idea as to how to handle this.'

'I'll get hold of him right away.'

'We released a preliminary article on the shooting in the park last night. You go ahead and run with this new information. I'll have Charise cover the briefing.'

Kari hated to give up anything to her most avid competitor, but this could turn out to be a much bigger story. 'OK, Scott. I'll get with Jason and we'll start looking into this right away.'

★ ★ ★

'We're in trouble. Big trouble!' Gloria ranted at Tony. 'That snoopy reporter was spying on me last night.'

'You mean Kari Underwood?' Tony was shocked. 'But how could she know anything?'

'That lying little sneak claimed Dom had run her off without a word, but he must have told her enough to make her curious about us. He might even have given her something to safeguard for him.'

'The photos!' Tony deduced fearfully. 'Say this isn't happening.'

'Tell Lincoln he needs to search that woman's apartment. We have to find those pictures.'

Tony hesitated. 'Uh, Chock doesn't want to risk going to her place again. He figures the cops will be watching it now.'

Gloria drummed her fingers on the desktop, emerald eyes flashing as she worked her brain for ideas. Suddenly she ceased moving, even breathing. Tony's eyes widened at the way she froze in thought.

'What?' he whispered, terrified of whatever shocking scheme she might have decided upon.

Gloria returned to an earthly plane, a hard set to her features. 'There's only one thing that will stop this investigation in its tracks. We need to tie everything together neatly and put an end to it.'

'Huh?' Tony was completely baffled. 'What are you talking about?'

'We didn't order the murder of Dom and Juno,' Gloria asserted. 'And we had nothing to do with Hector Gomez being shot and killed either.'

'Where are you going with this?'

Gloria put her radiant, intense eyes on him. 'This was all Chock Lincoln's doing. He deserves to face the death penalty for his crimes.'

'Yes, Glory honey, but if the police grab him, he'll rat us out in a minute!'

'Not if he doesn't get the chance.'

Tony backed away from her desk. 'I . . . I can't kill anyone. I could never do that!'

Gloria regarded the wimp with a combination of disbelief and disdain, as if she was sharing the room with the dumbest creature on the planet. However, she hid her disgust and asked, 'Do you still have the stuff from Dom's place and the guns Lincoln used?'

'Of course. I've got them hidden away where no one will find them.'

'Then this is what I want you to do.' She leaned forward, a grim determination on her face. Tony cringed at her somber demeanor, knowing he dared not defy this woman. Whatever her plan, he would do exactly what he was told.

★　★　★

Kari arrived at the precinct and found Jason with Detective Grady. They had been discussing the shooting from the previous night. Kari brought a new element to the table.

'Blackmail?' Grady was skeptical, after hearing her story. 'Someone probably sent that note to try and promote a host of new suspicions and keep us from finding out the truth.'

'What if it is the truth?' Kari asked. 'What if the killer was looking for blackmail materials of some kind?'

Jason looked at the note. It had been run off on an ordinary printer but he did take notice of one thing the others had missed. 'It's only an opinion, but this note appears to have been written by another solicitor, or someone intimate with a person in that profession.'

Grady and Kari both stared blankly at him for several seconds. 'Enlighten me,' Grady spoke first.

'Notice the wording of the last sentence — it reads one of *our* DDAs. A person outside the judicial system would have stated *one of the state's DDAs* or simply noted *a DDA* was involved.'

'It could have been a grammatical mistake,' Grady indicated. 'The author of this could have been in a hurry and not given much thought to the syntax he used.'

'Or it could have been the most natural way of writing the note.' Kari sided with Jason. 'If it was an unconscious admission . . . ' She didn't finish, but studied Grady for his honest reaction.

'This is an election year,' Grady pointed out. 'The contest for district attorney has been heating up for a few months now. Anything that might harm Gloria Streisand's grip on her office would be welcomed by Paul Hanson's camp.'

'You think this could have come from him or one of his supporters?' Kari wanted to know.

The detective cleared his throat. 'I think we might be making a big deal out of a single word. That said, blackmail would explain how come Dom and Juno had a lot of extra money lately, and why someone would search their house and steal their phones and computer.'

'And the part about a DDA?' Jason queried.

'Dom worked in the same state office building with Gloria and her assistants. He might have found some papers in the trash that were supposed to have been shredded. He could have overheard or seen something incriminating. Most people tend to ignore a janitor.'

'It would also explain why a paranoid person would be trying to frighten Kari away from the investigation,' Jason conjectured. 'They probably think Dom told her something that would lead her to uncovering the reason for the blackmail.'

'But they didn't tell me anything of importance,' Kari insisted. 'They practically threw me out of their house,'

'Someone thinks differently,' Jason said.

Kari removed the notepad from her purse. 'I wrote down everything I could remember, but Dom used so much gangsta slang I couldn't understand but every third or fourth word.'

Grady took a moment to look at her notes. 'Looks like poppycock to me too,' he agreed.

'Even so,' Jason said. 'Let me study it for a bit and see if I can make some sense from it.' He tore the page from Kari's notebook, folded it and stuck it inside his jacket pocket.

'Ham is talking to Rick Cory as we speak,' Grady told them. 'He is hoping Radar — his street informant — will know something about last night. Soon as Ham gets back we'll do some looking into this blackmail note. Without anyone knowing who sent it or who is involved, we can't do much.'

'We'll do a little snooping of our own,' Kari said. 'As the note was sent to me, I have every right to pursue the lead.'

Grady didn't try to talk her out of it. 'Take the Brit with you,' he said drily. 'I don't know if that will help you stay out of trouble or get the both of you in deeper, but at least you'll have company.'

They left the police station and Kari headed for her car.

'Do you have a plan?' Jason asked.

Kari smiled and said, 'Yes.'

* * *

The captain groaned and began to rub his temples as if suffering a migraine headache. 'Tell me this isn't happening,' he complained.

'Blackmail is what the note claimed,' Grady responded. 'Underwood and the Brit are on the scent. I went through the bank statements and phone records of Dom and Juno again. If they got a payoff from blackmail there should be a lot of cash, but I can't account for more than a couple thousand dollars. Add to that, the money they did deposit was over a period of several weeks.'

'They could have had a stash in the house,' the captain suggested. 'Maybe the killer found it.'

Hampton grunted his doubt. 'Doesn't fit the crime scene. There wasn't a single room untouched, meaning the shooter didn't stop searching until he had gone through the entire place. It would appear he didn't find what he was looking for. Plus, why take the computer and phones? Might get a few bucks for a laptop, but phones are worth practically nothing.'

'Couldn't this also mean Juno knew about the drug connection?' Captain Mercer questioned. 'And wouldn't passing that information along to the reporter make her a target?'

'I'm sure she isn't lying or holding anything back from us,' Grady assured him. 'Any information about the cartel, she would have recognized it. Blackmail, on the other hand, could be anything Dom might have said, some trifle she didn't even pick up on.'

Hampton put in his own two cents. 'Or it might be those two told her nothing at all, but our killer got nervous about her visit. He can't know for certain how much she knows.'

The captain was thoughtful for a time. 'We need a judge to sign off on us checking on this DDA angle. Considering the note implicates one of them, we need to pull their phone and bank records.'

'Westmoreland is eager for us to find his boy's killer,' Hampton reminded the captain. 'I'll bet he would give us the go ahead without involving the DA's office.'

Grady frowned. 'Do we dare go around her, Capt'n? She is not going to appreciate that kind of tactic.'

'This concerns someone on her staff, Grady. I think it's better if we leave her out of it for the time being. If something jumps out at us, we can clue her in for any further investigation.'

Hampton gave a nod. 'We'll head over and talk to Judge Westmoreland. Considering this may be a motive for his son's death, I don't think there will be any problem.'

'Keep me posted, gentlemen,' Captain

Mercer said. Then he walked back toward his office.

'I don't know, Ham,' Grady whispered. 'Now we don't trust the DA? Who's next, the Governor?'

Hampton snorted. 'Could happen. I didn't vote for him.'

15

They had to wait a few minutes, but Paul Hanson agreed to meet with Kari and Jason. They entered his office and sat down in standard chairs on one side of Paul's finely polished executive desk. He reclined back in a leather-bound executive's chair and offered a greeting smile.

Paul wore self assurance like his tailor-made suit, with cool, speculative eyes and the impassive expression of a high-stakes gambler. A man in his forties, clean shaven, still a full head of hair — neatly combed, but not professionally styled — he was a little above average in looks and appeared physically fit.

'So, Miss Underwood,' he greeted. 'We meet at last.'

'I'm flattered you know who I am.'

A practiced smile displayed perfectly straight, immaculate teeth. 'You needn't be coy. I am well aware of your part in bringing the Coin Killer to justice.' His eyes shifted to Jason. 'And you are her British counterpart.'

'Jason Keane,' he introduced himself.

Paul reached across the desk and shook his hand. Sitting back, he noticed the bulge under Jason's jacket and offered him a perplexed look. 'A visiting police officer from the UK who carries a gun? What kind of mission are you on?'

Jason made a dismissive gesture. 'The local detectives thought my being armed might be prudent. Miss Underwood has been targeted twice lately.'

'Yes, I heard about the shooting at the parking garage.' After a moment he grasped the second incident. 'And the attempted burglary at the West Jordan apartments — that was you who nearly caught the prowler?'

'Yes,' Jason replied. 'Had I been armed at the time, I could have arrested him.'

'So,' Paul said, proceeding to the purpose of their visit. 'What can I do for the two of you?'

'We'd like to know why you sent this letter to me,' Kari said confidently, holding out a copy of the bribe note. 'It was you, wasn't it?'

Paul took the paper, glanced at it and regarded her thoughtfully for a short time before answering. 'Why should I send something like that to you?'

'Because anyone wanting to discredit or investigate Gloria Streisand would know you have the most to gain should there be a scandal among her deputy attorneys.'

'Very astute . . . and accurate.' He praised her deduction, shocking them both. 'The letter was delivered to me in the same fashion as I had it passed along to you.'

Kari swallowed her surprise at his confession and forced her voice to work. 'Why me?' she managed in little more than a squeak.

The man gave her an impassive look. 'You said it yourself, I have the most to gain if this is true. Accordingly, it would be unethical for me to instigate an investigation on my own. I mean, what if Gloria herself should be implicated of complicity or wrongdoing? It would look like I had used this incident as an underhanded way to win the election.'

'So you thought of me?'

He stated, 'I knew you were the one reporter who would take the note seriously and see if there was any substance to the claim.'

'This could be from anyone who was jealous or vindictive toward the DA or any of her deputies,' Kari said.

Paul again paused, as if considering a number of options, before he selected the proper response. He was undoubtedly good at his job, weighing each word before speaking.

'If I had thought this was a malicious prank, I would have filed away the letter as an unsubstantiated rumor or slanderous refuse. But I happened upon an oddity some days ago that piqued my interest.'

'Something that could be related to blackmail?' Kari inquired.

Rather than declare a determination about the matter, he continued with his story. 'A career criminal named Chock Lincoln, who had been recently paroled, was picked up with a gun on his person. It was a clear violation of his parole and I would have expected to see him before a magistrate and be returned to prison.' Paul shook his head. 'Instead, the charge was dropped and he was released without a hearing.'

'Perhaps the circumstances . . . ' Jason began.

Paul gave his head a second shake. 'I looked into the matter. Mr. Lincoln claimed he was in fear for his life. Hence the need for a weapon.'

'That could be true,' Kari indicated.

'Lincoln had a reputation for always working alone. His record is two pages long and filled with a number of offenses. But he did not double-cross anyone, had no gang affiliations, and he was serving time for armed robberies and car theft. His victims were not the sort to seek violent retribution. In other words, I could see no justification for him to be carrying a weapon. There were no grounds for dismissing the charge.'

'Who managed to get the offense withdrawn?' Jason inquired.

'DDA Martin,' Paul replied. 'He is Mrs. Streisand's . . . ' he hesitated before adding, ' . . . number one assistant.'

Kari said, 'You think Lincoln may have had some kind of leverage on Martin and forced him to drop the charges?'

'Let's just say I didn't agree with the decision to let a violent felon walk free,' Paul acknowledged. He explained that Gloria had suggested the leniency was to prevent any racial bias charges; then he handed back the letter. 'And that is the reason I took this blackmail idea seriously. I have to wonder if Lincoln's release and the note are in some way related.'

'Do you have the original piece of mail?' Kari asked.

'I had both the paper and the self-sealing envelope dusted for prints. There was nothing on the standard page of paper and the only prints on the envelope belonged to my secretary, from when she found the letter in our box. It had no stamp, so it was hand delivered.'

'Then you have no idea of who might have sent the letter?'

'None whatsoever,' Paul replied. 'I'm sure they chose me because I am running against the current DA. Whoever it was didn't want to contact the police ... or perhaps they thought I would give the letter more credence than the police.'

'You do have the most to gain if Mrs. Streisand should be found guilty of a cover-up of some kind,' Kari implied.

Paul grinned. 'And that is exactly why I sent the note to you. I can't appear to be unscrupulously trying to dig up dirt on my opponent. That could cost me the very votes I need to win the election.'

Kari thanked him for seeing them and she and Jason left his office. Once outside, she locked her arm in his and headed for her car.

'What are your thoughts?' she asked, after a short way.

'That politics are no different in the States from what they are at home.'

She laughed. 'People are the same everywhere. It's all about greed, power and individual motivation.'

'We still have no idea as to who this blackmailer is, what the blackmail entails, and what he or she intends to gain.'

Kari said, 'We need to know if Dom and Juno were involved in this somehow. Being a janitor at the state building, Dom had access to sensitive papers and information.'

'There is also the money he and Juno had been spending lately,' Jason added. 'And someone did tear apart their place looking for something.'

'That's as much as we know, Detective Inspector Keane. What's our next move?'

'Give our detective friends a call about where the blackmail note came from and visit Juno's sister again?' Jason offered.

'You read my mind.'

He grinned. 'I am compelled to admit it makes remarkable reading.'

* * *

Hampton used his size to intimidate Ernie, towering over his desk, hands on his hips, as if he would snatch the man from his chair and start shaking him like rag doll.

'You had to wonder why Chock Lincoln was given a walk on a concealed weapons charge!' he bellowed. 'You are the man's parole officer!'

'He said he worked out some kind of deal,' Ernie whimpered impotently. 'I don't ask questions — I just do my job!'

'We did a little checking and discovered your brother-in-law had a DUI a few months back.' Grady took over. 'It would have been his fifth time for being caught driving under the influence. It usually means jail time after the third offense.'

'How did he get off . . . again?' Hampton joined in. 'Why did the DA's office give him a pass?'

'My sister has four kids, Detectives.' Ernie made the excuse. 'How is she going to take care of the family with her husband in jail?' He took a breath and added, 'He'd have lost his job, his house, his insurance, everything!'

'A drunk driver kills someone every forty-eight minutes in this country, nearly eleven thousand deaths a year.' Grady stated the latest published facts. 'We're talking innocent men, women and children. They lose more than their freedom for a few months, or their jobs and insurance . . . they lose their lives and the lives of their loved ones!'

'If you enjoy the security of your own job, you better stop jerking us around!' Hampton threatened. 'How did Lincoln get the weapons charge dropped?'

Ernie was in a panic. 'Look, I don't know all of the details!' he cried. 'DDA Martin asked me to let the paperwork go on Lincoln so the guy could have another chance to straighten out his life. Geez, Lincoln had only been back on the street for a few days.'

'And you did this favor for Martin because he didn't bring charges against your brother-in-law.' Grady summed up the conspiracy.

'Neither of these guys really deserved jail time,' Ernie sniveled. 'This was just a case of giving them one more chance to get their lives on track.'

Hampton glared at Ernie. 'I wouldn't get real comfortable with your job if I were you. If we track a major crime back to Lincoln . . . ' He didn't have to finish.

Grady walked at his side as the two of them left the building. On reaching the street Hampton paused to discuss their next move.

'That part checks out,' he said. 'Underwood's information was on target.'

'Still doesn't tell us who the blackmailer is.'

'We can go after Martin, but we need something more than a favor for Ernie and a show of compassion for a newly released parolee.'

'Let's do a little checking first, Ham. Maybe this Lincoln fellow is tied up with Dom or Juno? Maybe he knew them from before he went in the joint. It's possible that — '

Grady's cell rang, cutting his thought short. He glanced at the caller ID, told Hampton, 'The Captain,' and answered the call.

'Say what?' He gave Hampton a worried look. 'Yes, we'll get right on it.'

Soon as he finished speaking to their boss, Hampton asked, 'What gives?'

'Rick Cory's snitch contacted him a few minutes ago. He said someone has tagged Chock Lincoln as the shooter we're looking for.'

'You mean for all three killings?'

Grady bobbed his head. 'That's what the captain said.'

'How would his snitch find that out?'

'You remember, Cory told us about the guy everyone calls Radar. He's supposed to have more ears than a field of corn. He contacted Cory and said the news had just hit the streets.'

'You mean the gangs know too?'

Grady replied, 'Cory said the Hard Corps and Lobos are already searching for him. Big guy like Lincoln, covered in prison tattoos — he won't be hard to find.'

'Did you write down Lincoln's contact information?'

'Some dive over on Second West,' Grady said. 'But if he's behind the shootings, he won't have stayed in one place.'

'You're right, but we'd better check it out anyway . . . and I mean right now!'

★ ★ ★

It took a few minutes of visiting before Jason asked Mrs. Lovendaul to show him around her house again. She didn't seem to mind, happy for the company. Once they were out of the room, Kari told Rita about the blackmail scheme.

'Juno and Dom weren't involved in anything like that,' Rita said, defending them.

'The police will think so,' Kari insisted. 'They will label those two as extortionists and thieves.'

'They weren't breaking any laws.'

'So tell me, Rita, where were they getting their extra money?'

Rita sighed wearily. 'All right, I'll tell you the truth. It sounds as if it's the only way to keep the police from laying some phony blackmail charge on my brother.'

Kari waited for her to continue.

The girl turned around and lowered her voice, as if fearful Mrs. Lovendaul would overhear their conversation.

'It wasn't anything illegal or nothing,' she said firmly. 'I mean, Ida needed some work done on the house — a new carpet, the stairs fixed, a new storage shed . . . things like that.' Another pause, as if she were trying to figure the right way to word her explanation.

'I talked her into letting my brother and Dom do the work for her.' She barely took a breath and added: 'And they did a good job too. It wasn't real professional, but it wasn't a scam or nothing like that.'

'And you charged a little extra for the jobs?'

Rita ducked her head. 'It's not like Ida can't afford to be generous,' she said quietly. 'She was one of those seventy's feminists, you know, a women's lib sort, who lived only for a career.' Rita snorted her disgust. 'Well, she had her career, until she was too old to work and no one wanted her around any more. There ain't a soul alive who gives a darn if she lives or dies . . . except for me.' Rita's head came up and her voice grew cool with her own convictions. 'A family is something you can hold on to, Miss Underwood. If you haven't got a family, you haven't got nothing.'

'I believe in family.' Kari agreed with her.

'Well, Ida's got only me. I care for her, I really do. She treats me like her daughter, not a caregiver.'

'And you used her wealth to help Juno and Dom earn some extra money,' Kari concluded.

Rita's face worked, a mixture of shame and resolve. 'I was always up front with Ida about it,' she assured Kari. 'I told her what each job would cost. I even told her she might be able to get the chores done cheaper by someone else. But she said she was happy to help my brother and Juno. She offered to pay whatever I thought was fair.'

'That doesn't sound exactly ethical, but I doubt the police would consider it to be extortion.'

'No!' Rita said sharply. 'That's what I'm saying. Ida didn't mind paying a little extra to help out my brother. She liked Juno and Dom both. She always called them good boys and insisted I make them lunch or take them cold drinks while they were working on a project.'

'And your new car?' Kari asked. 'Is she helping you with that too?'

Rita sighed. 'I didn't ask her to buy it for me. But I often had to take a bus to get here, because my old junker kept breaking down. She wanted me to move in with her, but I didn't feel right about that.' She gestured with an open hand. 'Maybe, down the road, if something happens and Ida can't get around good. She's scared of not being able to tend to herself and being locked away in a nursing home.' Rita put on a stern expression. 'I've promised her I won't let that happen.'

Jason returned from his tour of the house and Kari told him that she was finished with the interview. They both thanked Mrs. Lovendaul and Rita, then left the house.

'Well, I've cleared up where Dom and Juno

were getting their extra money,' Kari told Jason, as soon as they were in the car. 'They were doing odd jobs for Mrs. Lovendaul.'

'I saw their handiwork.'

'Bad?' Kari worried.

'Not precisely first rate, but most of their chores were adequate. The new storage shed — which Mrs. Lovendaul didn't appear to need — was quite well done. The carpet, stairs and new bathroom sink are not professional quality, but they are satisfactory.'

'I'd hate to think Rita was taking advantage of a senior citizen, but she seems to truly care for the woman.'

'I agree,' Jason said. 'When I suggested the work might have been available at a lesser price, Mrs. Lovendaul stated how she preferred to help out a couple of young men who were living on their own.'

'We better let the detectives know where Dom and Juno got their money. It will eliminate the boys as potential blackmailers.'

'I also wish to speak to them . . . ' at Kari's sharp glance, he grinned and finished, 'just to see how the case is going.'

16

Tony burst into Gloria's office, his face pale and eyes wide with trepidation. Gloria wondered if Dotty had even bothered to ask his business, but he likely claimed it was an emergency.

'Close the door,' she ordered him stiffly, stopping him before he could run over and throw himself down to grovel at her feet.

Tony recovered his composure enough to make sure the door was securely fastened. Then he hurried over to stand opposite of her at the desk.

'The cops got to Ernie!' he began, unable to control the quiver in his voice. 'He told them about me!'

'Relax, Tony,' Gloria used a soothing voice, as if speaking to an alarmed child. 'It's taken care of.' Then she enlightened him about how she had already cleared up the event with Paul Hanson. 'I told him the DA's office did not want to appear racist and allowing Lincoln a second chance was an act of benevolence.'

'Did Hanson buy it?' Tony wanted to know. 'I mean, Lincoln had a list of arrests as long as your arm. He's hardly anyone the public would want us to give another chance to.'

'It was my call, so it had nothing to do with you. If the police come asking questions, you refer them to me.'

Tony heaved a breath of relief. 'This is all so nerve-racking. The blackmail, the murders, the inquiries . . . everything.'

'We just have to keep our heads. If things go as planned today, everything will be wrapped up in one neat package. The ordeal will be finished.'

Tony nodded hopefully. 'I had to sit outside Lincoln's place for four hours, but he finally went out for something to eat.'

'Did you get everything planted?'

'So long as the guy doesn't look under his bed. There's not a lot of hiding places in that rundown motel room.'

Gloria looked at her watch. 'It's quitting time. I've got to get home. Don is off work today and is fixing me supper.' She groaned. 'I think he's actually trying to win my affections back.'

'You're not even sleeping together,' Tony pointed out. 'Isn't he making the effort a little too late?'

'I can't divorce him until I win re-election. After that we're done.' She waved a dismissive hand. 'If the court awards him half of my worth, that's what I'll surrender. I want all of this behind me.'

'What about us, Glory honey?' Tony asked. 'I can't leave my wife.'

Gloria almost told him the truth: that she intended to clean house among her staff and replace him, that there would be no more *us*! However, she needed the simpering dog to remain loyal until her re-election was secured. With a warm smile, she said: 'Not to worry, Tony. We'll still have time for each other.'

★   ★   ★

Peggy's voice came over the air on the radio. 'Grady? Ham? Are you in your car?'

Hampton grabbed the receiver and pushed the transmit button. 'We're here, Dispatch. Go ahead.'

'Captain Mercer says for you two to stop by the motel at 1350 South and Main Street. See the manager about a weapon found in one of the rooms.'

'10-4, Dispatch. We're on our way.'

Grady was already turning that direction. 'It's got to be Lincoln,' he said.

'No doubt about it. With all of the media scanners, Peg knew better than to put any information over the air.'

'If sector cars were dispatched it's likely the news people will have someone there already.'

They were two blocks away when they saw no fewer than six police cars. Two television station vans were also parked near by, along with an ambulance and several other official looking vehicles.

'It didn't do much good for your girlfriend to try and keep this quiet,' Grady said. 'We seem to be the only ones in the entire valley who isn't already on the scene.'

A uniformed policeman recognized the detectives and signaled to a place they could park. Two cops were stringing yellow caution tape to mark off about a hundred feet in three directions from one corner motel room.

The detectives exited the car and were met by Rick Cory from the gang unit. His presence was enough to tell them they had found their prime suspect too late.

'How bad?' Hampton asked Cory.

'There's a lot of blood, but it probably all belongs to the vic, Chock Lincoln. It looks as if he was caught while in the shower. From the witness reports, everything happened very quickly. Several gang members arrived and a couple roughed up the clerk and got the room number for Lincoln. They surrounded his room, went through both of the windows and smashed in the front door, all at the same time. After the crashing of glass and the door, there was some shouting and cussing, but no shooting. One woman said she saw at least a dozen gang members running from the room, after the attack. They were all wearing hoods and gloves. She said a couple appeared to be carrying clubs.'

'I imagine it goes without saying that Lincoln is dead?' Grady spoke up.

'A man falling into a hamburger grinder wouldn't have looked worse,' Cory told the two detectives. 'I'll bet every bone in his body is broke.'

'Peg . . . um . . . Dispatch said something about a gun?' Hampton probed.

'The uniforms found a nine millimeter handgun and a .308 hunting rifle with a scope.' He let the news sink in. 'There was also a laptop computer, matching the description of the one taken from Juno and Dom's house.'

'But Lincoln didn't have a chance to get off a shot?' Hampton asked.

'The items were still under his bed when we arrived on the scene. Lincoln never got out of the bathroom.'

Grady and Hampton exchanged knowing looks. It was Hampton who spoke. 'All tied up in a neat little package.' He snorted his contempt. 'Could this be any more obvious?'

'Lincoln is a likely suspect for the shooting, Ham. He fits the profile, and if he has a ski mask . . . ?'

'You mean one of those expensive types, made of Neoprene?' Cory asked. At the curious looks of the two detectives, he gave an affirmative nod. 'It was in a dresser drawer, plus gloves and a black-hooded sweatshirt.'

'He's our man,' Grady proclaimed. 'Whether he was set up or got careless, he's our shooter, our thief, and our prowler who fought with the Brit.'

'Why shoot at the reporter?' Cory asked the question.

Hampton surmised, 'She saw him outside of Dom and Juno's house. He must have thought she could ID him.'

'We still have the note about blackmail,' Grady asserted. 'Who was blackmailing whom? And about what?'

Cory laughed. 'Damn, you guys want answers to everything, don't you?' He patted Hampton on the back. 'Did you ever hear the saying about not looking a gift horse in the mouth?'

'This is one horse whose teeth I'm going to count.' Hampton growled his reply.

Cory said 'see ya' and walked away as another cop approached. This one had a notepad in his hand.

'Got a little more on the attackers,' he told them. 'One witness, who swears he won't testify, said the gangs were wearing two different colors. The arm — or head-bands and other gang colors match both the 39th Street Lobos and the Hard Corps.'

'Well there's something positive, Ham,' Grady avowed with a sardonic expression. 'It appears the truce is still in play!'

Hampton dismissed the humor. 'Let's check the crime scene and pick up the weapons, computer and clothing. It's time to put this case to bed.'

★   ★   ★

Jason took over watching the pork chops and frying potatoes on the stove top, while Kari scribbled some notes and got information over the telephone from Detective Grady. When she finished talking to him, she returned to see how the food was coming.

'It's easy to see you've been living a bachelor's life,' she praised. 'Nothing burned and all of it ready to put on the table.'

'I don't do a lot of cooking,' Jason admitted. 'It's a lonely chore to sit down and eat by one's self, even with the telly blaring away for company.'

Once they were seated at the table and eating, Kari explained about the gang attack at the motel and the death of Chock Lincoln. She covered the evidence linking him to the three murders, plus the shooting at her car and him being the man Jason fought with outside her apartment.

'It's a rare event when the police are handed a case where a number of crimes are solved and the guilty party is executed all at the same time.'

'The case isn't solved,' Kari contradicted. 'There's still the matter of blackmail.'

'Except no one knows what the blackmail is about or who was the target.'

'Details, details,' Kari quipped.

'I heard you talking to Grady. Didn't he tell you they had looked into phone and bank records of the DDAs?'

Kari displayed a thoughtful frown. 'Yes. He said none of the deputy district attorneys had withdrawn any large amount of cash, and there were only a few untraceable phone calls.' She paused to point her fork at Jason. 'So maybe this wasn't about money at all.'

'Let's follow the trail and see where it leads,' Jason suggested.

'This all appears to have started shortly

223

after Chock Lincoln was picked up with a concealed weapon,' she began. 'He gets off because a DDA makes the charge go away.'

'And no complaint from the parole officer,' Jason reminded her.

'Then Grady discovers the parole officer owed a favor to the same DDA for helping his brother-in-law avoid prosecution for a driving-under-the-influence charge.'

'Yes, but why did the DDA want to help Lincoln?'

Kari was chewing on a bite of pork and skewed her expression again. It took a concentrated effort for Jason to keep from smiling. Watching her, it appeared as if Kari's brain was working to process the facts from every angle imaginable. When she swallowed the mouthful, she again waved the fork.

'You're absolutely right, Jason. We need to talk to DDA Martin. He's the one who started this chain of events. Paul Hanson said Gloria didn't want to face any racial bias over revoking Lincoln's parole. The question is, was that her idea or was it at Martin's suggestion?'

'Because one of them might have had a reason of their own,' Jason deduced.

'We still don't know why Lincoln went after Juno and Dom. What was he looking for?' She took a breath, puzzled. 'And why shoot at me and then try to break into my apartment? What am I supposed to know or have in my possession?'

'We have a good many questions and only a dead man for answers, love. Where do we go from here?'

'I think we need to view this case like a ladder. Lincoln is the bottom step, the one who did the dirty work. Next comes Ernie, but his motive is a debt to Martin. We should start with Martin and see where that leads.'

'I agree with everything except your bottom rung of the ladder.' At Kari's inquiring look, Jason clarified. 'The first step might well be the blackmail.'

'You're right . . . unless the letter was sent only as a ruse to throw us off track.'

'That's also a possibility,' Jason agreed. 'But we can't know that until we find out who sent it.'

'At least I'm no longer a target,' Kari said carefully. Then with a worried look, 'Does that mean you'll be leaving me?'

'Not until we know if this case is over and *why* you were a target,' he assured her. 'I intend to be a bother for a while longer.'

That put a bright smile on her face. 'I'm liable to hire someone to threaten me just to keep you here.'

Jason laughed. 'I believe we've enough of a

problem trying to solve this mystery instead. I'd as soon not be grappling with intruders and having you dodge any more bullets.'

'We'll keep it simple then. As soon as I attend the police briefing and write my story, we will go find out what Martin has to say.'

★ ★ ★

Gloria entered the judge's chambers and found him sitting at his desk. He looked years older than he had a mere week earlier. The death of his son had hit him harder than she would have expected. Garth had always complained that Dom was shiftless, trouble-some and too lazy to improve himself with college. Obviously their personal rift did not go so far as to a lack of love for the boy.

'I suppose you saw the news last night?' Gloria said. 'Chock Lincoln is the man who killed Dom and Juno. Then he shot Hector Gomez so it would look like two gangs were at war. The handgun found in his room matched the bullets fired in both killings and the rifle is the one he used to shoot at the reporter.'

'What motive did he have for shooting at her?' Judge Westmoreland asked.

'She saw him sitting in his car, a short way up the street from Juno and Dom's house. He

226

must have thought she could identify him.'

'So the investigation is over?'

'Yes.'

'And the blackmail?' the judge queried.

Gloria was stunned to silence. Her heart ceased to beat and the breath left her lungs. She struggled to regain enough poise and wind to gasp out the single word, 'Blackmail?'

Westmoreland waved his hand. 'Oh, forgive me, I wasn't supposed to say anything. It doesn't concern you at the moment.'

Gloria's mind raced. 'Blackmail always concerns a DA, Your Honor,' she said professionally, recovering a degree of calm in both her voice and demeanor. 'Does this have to do with Dom and Juno? Is that why their phones and computer were taken — someone accused them of blackmail?'

'It's a moot point now, Gloria. The case is closed. The killer of my boy is dead.'

'Certainly. I understand.'

As she stood expectantly, Westmoreland expounded a bit more. 'There was an anonymous letter sent to the police, via the same reporter whom Lincoln took a shot at. It suggested someone in your office was involved in blackmail, one of your deputy attorneys. I'm sure it is nothing to worry about. As far as I know, the police found nothing to indicate there was any wrongdoing by your people.'

'That's a relief.'

'Forget I mentioned it,' he said. Then, after thinking on it for a moment, 'Let the police finish their internal investigation and put the matter to rest.'

'Of course, Your Honor,' Gloria replied. 'I won't say a word.'

Westmoreland offered her a jaded smile. 'Thank everyone for finding my son's killer. It doesn't fill the empty place in my heart, but it is a relief to know the murderer is no longer at large.'

'I'll pass your gratitude along to the detectives,' Gloria vowed. Then she said her goodbye and left the office.

As soon as she reached the hallway she dug out the acid relief pills in her purse. A blackmail note! Who the hell could have sent a blackmail note?

17

Kari attended the briefing and returned to her office to write up the story of Chock Lincoln — his crimes and his death. Jason didn't go with her, but chose to visit the lead detectives at their office.

Grady, seated at his desk was, as usual, the more communicative of the two. Hampton stood a few feet away, less than eager to share information with any outsider. Fortunately, he did not openly resent Jason's interest in their case.

'You're saying both gangs were involved in the attack against Chock Lincoln?' Jason posed the question to Grady.

'Yeah, it smells to high heaven, but we've got nothing else. The gang unit said the news hit the street yesterday afternoon. By the time the information got to us, both the Lobos and the Hard Corps had sent a few of their soldiers to visit Lincoln. They caught him in the shower and beat him to death.'

'You had no joy in finding this character, but the two gangs knew where to look. Does that not strike you odd?'

'Everything about this strikes us odd,'

Hampton growled, breaking his silence. 'We've been taken down a merry walk like a baby in a buggy! This was an orchestrated hit! Someone knew where Lincoln was staying and planted the weapons and computer in his room.'

'Planted?'

'They were under his bed, but all three items were completely free of fingerprints. Who wipes incriminating evidence clean and then hides it under his bed?'

'Even so, you believe he is responsible for the killings?'

'Found his mask and gloves,' Grady said. 'There were a couple strands of his hair embedded in the mask and we found gunpowder residue on the gloves and his shirt. We even matched blood from Dom and Juno on his shoes. Yeah, he was the killer all right.'

'Do you have an explanation for the absence of prints on the weapons or computer?'

'It's like Ham said, they were planted.'

'So Chock Lincoln may have had a partner in crime and that person did the double-cross,' Jason postulated.

'We've nothing but guesswork,' Grady admitted. 'It's possible Lincoln wiped everything down because he intended to dump the evidence later.'

'There is still the blackmail note. Have you uncovered anything positive along that line of inquiry?'

'We did link one DDA indirectly to Chock Lincoln, but we've no evidence the two men ever met.' He explained about DDA Martin and Ernie, the way the two had done favors for one another. He also said DA Streisand had stated she did not want to charge Lincoln because she feared there might be some racial backlash. He finished with, 'We checked the records of all of the DDAs and found nothing. Martin had made a couple calls to a throwaway phone, but we can't tie that in with Lincoln.'

'What about the DA herself?'

'You trying to get us fired?' Grady carped. 'She and Judge Westmoreland are good friends. No way he would sign off on checking her phone and bank records,'

'Might I suggest you go to someone else.'

Hampton stepped over to stand behind Grady. 'All right, Brit.' His tone was rigid. 'What do you know that we don't?'

'Actually, I don't *know* anything,' Jason admitted. 'But your lady DA has shown signs of — let's call it *curious* behavior. Her interviews with Miss Underwood have closely resembled interrogations.'

'A woman with power is often a little

overbearing.' Grady excused her aggressive tendencies. 'Plus, she was bound to be anxious to solve the death of Judge Westmoreland's son.'

'I accept duty or friendship might be her motivation,' Jason accepted. 'But she and DDA Martin seem to share a rather cozy rapport — perhaps even an intimate relationship.'

Hampton skewed his face in a scowl. 'You know this for a fact?'

'It's more of an assumption from their mutual behavior.'

'You mean a hunch,' Hampton proclaimed.

Grady was also skeptical. 'That's all you have?'

'You just informed me that it was DDA Martin who dealt with the parole officer responsible for Lincoln not being charged for carrying a weapon. DA Streisand backs up his story by insisting the action was taken to pacify any racial organizations from accusing her of bias. What if the real reason for helping Mr. Lincoln was blackmail?'

Hampton and Grady looked at one another. 'I don't know.' Grady was the one to speak. 'You're treading on very thin ice, Keane.'

'And if that ice breaks, me and Grady could end up walking a beat again,' Hampton agreed. 'We would be kissing our careers goodbye if we pulled the DA's records and found nothing.'

'I understand,' Jason told the two men. 'The blackmail note could be a fraudulent decoy, intended to dissuade you from following the correct line of inquiry. It's possible there might never have been any blackmail at all.'

'We will take your assumption to the captain and see what he thinks,' Hampton promised. 'Don't hold your breath for a warrant.'

'Thank you for entertaining Miss Underwood's and my thoughts on this matter,' Jason said, ending his visit. 'Always a treat talking to you chaps.'

'And you never cease to add to our headaches,' Hampton shot back. 'I'd wager the stock price on painkiller goes up in this country every time you visit.'

The three of them laughed and Jason left the office.

★　★　★

Kari was about to send her article to the editor's desk when Jason walked up to her cubicle.

'I hope I'm not being a bother, love,' he

apologized. 'I just left the detectives and didn't have anything else to occupy my time.'

'I'm about done here. The story is ready to — ' She was interrupted by the phone ringing. She answered and discovered the caller was Rick Cory. Asking him to hold for a moment, she informed Jason of who was on the line. He remembered her telling him that Cory was the lead officer in the gang unit.

'I'm told you had a busy night last night,' she began the conversation with Cory. 'Two gangs working together to kill a mutual enemy? That must be a first.'

'And no witnesses saw anything . . . on the record,' Rick replied.

'Anything new on the Colombian drugs?'

'My source has confirmed that the shooting at Liberty Park was related to the cartel. Those two bangers from the Lobos are lucky to be alive.'

'Still no idea who the cartel is dealing with?'

'No clue at all, Kari. I'm thinking they might not be working with a gang at all. This might be a single dealer, someone who knows the different gangs and can sell to them all.'

'That's a scary thought.'

'Do you have your story written about Lincoln's demise yet?'

'I'm about finished,' Kari said. 'Is there

anything you'd like me to add?'

'Only that someone tipped off both gangs, *before* my source got the information to me. That's the reason I was there. Radar contacted me as to the whereabouts of Chock Lincoln, but by the time I got over there it was all over.'

'Did Radar tell you how he found out about the hiding-place?'

'You know how informants work, they listen, they dole out a little cash for tidbits of information. Sometimes it pans out and we get lucky and sometimes we get the information too late.'

'I understand.'

'How about you and your pal?' Rick asked. 'Are you two any closer to finding this elusive drug connection?'

'We've chased a few leads but have nothing concrete.'

'You be careful about where you tread,' Rick warned. 'Those guys play for keeps.'

'I'll be careful,' Kari promised.

'If I find anything worthwhile I'll be in touch,' Rick said. 'I've got a wife and daughter who live in this valley. We both have to keep trying to stop the drug traffic and make our streets safer.'

'You're a good man, Rick. I wish I could do a story on you, so everyone would know how much we all owe to the gang unit. Your work is dangerous and there aren't a lot of rewards for your efforts.'

'That's us, the silent heroes, the ones you don't hear about.'

Jason motioned for her to give him the phone and she asked, 'Can I put you on with my partner in crime detection?'

'Certainly. Anything I can do to help.'

'Officer Cory,' Jason said and introduced himself. 'I wonder if you would grant me the benefit of your street education?'

'Shoot,' Cory replied. 'How can I help?'

Jason removed a piece of paper from his jacket and asked, 'Can you give me the definition of the following terms: *hitting it*; getting *baked*; and someone who is referred to as a *fizzle*?'

Cory gave him the street interpretation for each and asked, 'You aren't thinking of going undercover as a gang banger?'

Jason laughed at the idea. 'Hardly that. I do thank you for your help.'

'No problem. Keep our reporter out of harm's way.'

'I'll certainly do my best. Goodbye.'

'Are you trying to decode my notes?' Kari wanted to know, as she put the phone back on its cradle.

'It's possible that Dom told you more than

you realized.' He tucked the paper away. 'I'll work on it later.'

'Then you have nothing to add to my story?' At the negative shake of his head, she clicked the mouse on the 'Send' icon on her computer. 'Then I'm finished for the day. Let's get out of here.'

★ ★ ★

Gloria was scanning a list of cases on her desk when Dotty's voice came over the intercom on her desk.

'Call on line one for you, Gloria. It's Judge Westmoreland.'

Gloria grabbed up the phone at once. 'Garth — Your Honor,' she changed hastily. 'I didn't expect a call from you, not after our visit to your office. What's going on?'

'I got a rather troublesome call a few minutes ago, Gloria,' (he didn't concern himself about title proprieties). 'Captain Mercer was inquiring as to whether the warrant I issued for your deputy DA's bank and telephone records included you.'

'Me?' Gloria was aghast. 'Why should anyone want to snoop into my accounts and phone records?'

'It's that ridiculous blackmail note,' Westmoreland replied. 'I told them I shouldn't have issued the warrant at all, not when our only source of information was an anonymous note. It was my grief over losing Dom.' He excused his action. 'I was desperate to find out why he was killed.'

'I understand completely,' Gloria assured him, fearful he would ask her to give permission to look at her accounts. Quickly, trying to head off any such request, she stated: 'Our own office has come to the conclusion that Lincoln somehow learned Dom and Juno had come into some money recently. His intent in going to their house was to rob them. We know he discarded or sold their phones and iPad, and he probably intended to sell the computer. He had bought some clothes for cash, paid for his room with cash, and we think he had a considerable amount of money in his room. How much we don't know, as the gang members who killed him took whatever money they found. The only things they left behind were the weapons and computer.'

'Hard to believe gang members would leave guns behind.'

'We think it's because they were in a rush to get away before the cops arrived. It's likely none of them stopped to look under the bed, because they were there for revenge's sake — to even the score for Lincoln killing

Hector, Dom and Juno.'

'Do the police have any suspects for Lincoln's murder?'

'No, and the assailants were all wearing gloves and ski masks. I doubt we'll find any of the killers, unless we happen to get a confession from one of the gang somewhere down the road.'

'Then, as far as you're concerned, this case is closed?'

'Yes, Your Honor.'

'Fine. I believe it's best if we continue with our lives and put this all behind us.'

'I'm sorry you lost your son over such a simple case of greed. Lincoln could have robbed Juno and Dom and been done with it. There was no reason to kill those boys.'

'Thank you for your time, Gloria. I'll be seeing you.'

'Of course. Good day, Your Honor.'

When the line went dead, Gloria immediately rang Martin's office. He agreed to meet her after lunch, as he was due in court for a preliminary hearing on a hit-and-run case. She didn't tell him what the meeting was about, knowing he might fall apart and not be able to perform the duties of his office.

Then she sat back and began to rub her forehead. Would this never end? If Captain Mercer had asked Westmoreland about the warrant, his office must still be looking into the blackmail angle. She swore under her breath and lamented, 'Why can't anything work out the way I planned?'

★ ★ ★

Jason and Kari found themselves in an imbroglio. The police were unable to pursue a blackmail angle, having no leverage for a warrant to look into the DA's personal financial records. To this point in time, they had recovered no incriminating evidence to support the blackmail theory.

As for speaking to DDA Martin, he had managed to dodge their visits and was not taking Kari's phone calls. Deciding to take a more direct approach, they ambushed him as he was leaving the court room.

'Chock Lincoln's parole officer said you were the one who talked him into dropping the weapons charge.' Kari challenged him with what information they had. 'Now that he has been identified as a multiple murderer, do you think this will be used against Gloria Streisand in the upcoming election?'

Martin was rattled, but he had a lawyer's instincts. 'It was considered a worthwhile effort at the time. No one can foresee the future when it comes to dealing with dangerous felons.'

'You admit he was dangerous.' Jason pounced on his term. 'Yet you chose to intervene on his behalf. I daresay a person convicted of a minor drug or theft conviction would have seemed more worthy of your efforts.'

'Fifteen arrests.' Kari outlined Lincoln's offenses. 'And he had a history of numerous assaults, car thefts and burglaries. Hardly the borderline case of someone who made a single mistake.'

Martin had no reply, so Jason suggested, 'Perhaps Lincoln was to return the favor in some way. He was tough, intimidating, physical — '

'No!' Martin snapped. 'You're trying to pin some kind of rap on me and I won't have it!' He spun toward Kari. 'If you have questions to ask, make an appointment with my secretary. Don't be pestering me while I'm in the middle of doing my job.'

Kari displayed complete innocence. 'We only asked you about a case in which you are a person of interest.'

'I'm not a person of interest in anything!' Martin cried. 'I relayed the department's concern about how it might look to return a man to prison within a few days of his release. Lincoln claimed he was concerned for his life. He was only protecting himself.'

'Against whom?' Jason wanted to know. 'What did Mr. Lincoln have to fear?'

'I don't know. It was none of my business.'

'Oh, but it was!' Kari fired at him. 'You are the one who got him released. Your name is listed as the contact who requested Ernie not to revoke Lincoln's parole. You are involved whether you like it or not.'

Martin began to walk faster, hurrying to escape. Kari and Jason kept pace and she renewed her verbal assault.

'Someone tipped off the gangs as to where Mr. Lincoln was hiding,' Kari hammered at him. 'Were you privy to where he was staying?'

'No!'

'According to the word on the street, his whereabouts was leaked to both Jesse Ventura and Victor Orozco. Who else could have known where he was?'

'I told you, if you want to talk to me, do it properly by making an appointment with my office.' Martin did not hide his anger — and anxiety at her line of questioning. 'However, this gangland violence is not my responsibility and I won't discuss it any further.'

Kari and Jason let the man go. He was practically running for the door.

'That ought to get a reaction from Gloria,' Kari said, wearing a crooked little smile.

'He is definitely hiding something,' Jason said. 'Did you notice? He actually paled at the question of who might have contacted the two gang leaders.'

'According to Rick Cory, it was an anonymous tip.'

'A tip that happened to reach the gangs a full hour or more before Cory and the police got the same information.'

'This isn't over yet,' Kari vowed. 'I'm convinced the blackmail fits into this somewhere.'

Jason adjusted his shoulder holster and smoothed his suit jacket. 'I'll be glad to be rid of this firearm,' he said. 'It's rather cumbersome to carry about.'

Kari grinned and wrinkled her nose. 'It might be troublesome, but it's a tremendous vote of confidence from our police department. That ought to make you feel special.'

Jason couldn't argue. He returned a smile and replied, 'Quite.'

18

Grady put down the phone as the captain approached his desk. As usual, Hampton rotated about in his chair so that he would also be available for orders or conversation.

'If I can no longer hear out of my right ear,' the captain began, 'It's because DA Streisand has been screaming in it at the top of her lungs for the last ten minutes!'

'What's got her pantyhose in a twist?' Hampton wondered. 'She ought to be singing praises about us closing the case on two shootings and an attempted break-in.'

'It seems Miss Underwood and the Brit have been making nuisances of themselves. They confronted DDA Martin and insinuated he was somehow responsible for Lincoln's actions and possibly his demise as well.'

Grady groaned. 'Capt'n, we can't control the press . . . especially our resident Lois Lane.'

'It's true,' Hampton joined in with their defense. 'The reporter has her own ideas about this case and there isn't a thing we can do to change her mind.'

'You mean the blackmail?'

'A lot of things don't add up,' Grady said. 'We've no motive for why Lincoln killed Juno or Dom; we get a tip-off about his whereabouts . . . long after both gang leaders were contacted, and we find a stash of loot and weapons that link Lincoln to the murders, except they are wiped clean of fingerprints!'

'Then we have the letter about blackmail too,' Hampton added to the enigma. 'I don't know about you, but Grady and me hate being manipulated like a couple of hand puppets!'

Captain Mercer folded his arms, resolute, yet his features were pensive. 'The thing is, men, Gloria wants this case closed and is about one breath away from filing a restraining order against Kari Underwood.'

Hampton harrumphed at the idea. 'Never happen. That would be handing over a truckload of ammunition to Paul Hanson. He could campaign on her abuse of power and denying the freedom of the press. She'd be a fool to actually follow through with something like that.'

The captain remained in a bind. 'What am I supposed to do? I can't side with the reporter against our own DA, yet I can't support the DA's demand that I intervene and stop Underwood from investigating something we ought to be investigating ourselves.'

'Let us try and work this out with the Brit and Kari,' Grady suggested. 'Maybe we can smooth this over enough to keep it from blowing up in all of our faces.'

'We could put this all to rest if Gloria Streisand would allow us to look at her financial and phone records,' Hampton said. 'The woman is hiding something. Why else would she get so uptight over a few questions from a reporter? Especially questions that were not directed at her?'

'I've tried my best,' the captain informed them. 'I asked the judge about a warrant and he said absolutely not. He didn't feel we had enough evidence to support an investigation into something that might be a hoax and seems unlikely to have a bearing on our case at hand. He's satisfied Chock Lincoln killed his boy during a robbery and then tried to make it look like part of a gang feud. In his mind, this is over and done with.'

'What are your orders?' Grady asked the captain.

Captain Mercer took a stance. 'Keep doing what you're doing. But warn the reporter to stay away from the DA or her people, until such time as they have some hard evidence.'

As her paramour approached her desk, Gloria waved Martin to take a seat. She didn't feel like having him slobbering over her at the moment. He docilely took a chair and waited for her to speak.

'I told you to refer the reporter or anyone else who questioned our actions to me,' she began in a scolding tone of voice. 'Now that nosy reporter has the police breathing down my neck. Underwood's incessant interference has me so wired that I up and threatened to get a restraining order against her.' She swore vehemently and buried her face in her hands. 'How did this situation get so completely screwed up? It's like being stuck in a soggy, slimy mire, and the more you struggle and try to get out, the more you are sucked deeper into the muck.'

'I didn't tell them anything,' Martin mumbled, sniveling weakly. 'I told you every word that was said when I called you. It's just that . . . well, I think they have guessed the truth!'

'Don't be ridiculous, Tony. They don't know anything.'

'They know enough to want a look at your records,' he insisted. 'And Judge Westmoreland told you about the police getting a warrant for my phone and financial accounts.'

'Yes,' Gloria admitted. 'Garth inadvertently let that slip, but the action was taken before Chock Lincoln's death and they came up empty.'

'What are we going to do?'

Gloria regarded him with a critical gaze. What had she ever seen in him? He was a moderately competent prosecutor, but as a human being he was a whimpering, spineless weakling. He had been eager to taste the forbidden fruit Gloria offered in an adulterous affair, but he lacked the fortitude and strength of a real man. He had been an affectionate lover, but it was his sole redeeming character trait.

'This has to end,' Gloria vowed. 'I can't have a reporter looking over my shoulder while I'm running my re-election bid. She is bound to find something Hanson can use against me.'

'What do you think happened to your fifty thousand dollars?' Martin asked. 'You think Dom and Juno hid it where it couldn't be found?'

'I don't know. Maybe Lincoln found the money and kept it for himself. If he did, the gang members probably stole it from his motel room.'

'And the pictures?'

Gloria scowled. How could she possibly know more than he did? Sometimes she hated herself for ever cheating on Don. He was not attentive to her needs and had wrongly assumed that, because they both worked, it meant there was a degree of equality about their marriage. *Except I paid for our house and two cars; I'm the one who inherited a fortune from my father!*

'Dom must have done as he promised and erased the photos,' she said, hopefully.

'If he did, then what about the note? Who could have sent the letter about the blackmail to the reporter?'

How can I possibly know that? she about screamed at him. Instead, she held her temper in check and stuck to the problem at hand. 'Our single concern at the moment is how to get Underwood and her British pal off of our backs.'

Martin sighed impotently. 'Too bad she didn't find out some crucial information about the drug cartel, the one she wrote about. I'll bet they would have known how to deal with her!'

Gloria stared at him in amazement, as his casual statement sparked the glimmer of an idea. The notion caused her pulse to race. 'Yes, the Colombian North Valley drug cartel. I remember her story.'

'Supposed to be distributing drugs to nearly every gang and dealer in the valley,' Martin went on offhandedly. 'The commissioner said he had people looking into the rumor, but I'm betting the only ones doing any real undercover work is the special gang unit.'

Gloria felt a rush of adrenaline. The burst of raw energy compelled her to stand up and begin pacing the floor. She wrung her hands anxiously, turning ideas over in her head.

'Who did you tip off about Lincoln's location?' she asked, after two complete circles of the room.

'You remember that ditzy blonde — I let her off on a prostitution and possession charge a month or so back, the one with snake tats on her neck?'

'Selene or something?'

'She's the one,' he said. 'When I interviewed her, she said she knew a lot of bangers, including the gang unit's snitch . . . Radar.' He paused, but Gloria's smoldering stare warned that she wanted more information. Martin hurried to continue. 'I told her to put the word on the street so the Lobos and Hard Corps could take care of our problem.'

'Who all did she tell?'

'I'm not sure.'

'You didn't tell her about Radar's connection to the gang unit?'

'Of course not.' He looked almost offended. 'I told her to spread the word about Lincoln's location. And when I asked if she knew anyone special, she brought up his name. He's the one who called Rick Cory.'

'Do you think Selene has any idea as to who is working for the cartel?'

Martin blinked in confusion. 'Not to name names, but she did say the cartel people seem to know everything that's happening in the valley.'

'Yes, they moved the location for their last exchange to Liberty Park. That's not a place they would normally use, unless they feared someone was watching them or their usual hangouts.'

'What good does that do us?' Martin asked. 'We have no information on who is handling their deals from either end. It's a total mystery to the police.'

Gloria walked over and stared out the window of her second-story office. She could see the busy street below, with people walking around as if without a care in the world. How wonderful that must feel. This burden of guilt had grown until she couldn't eat or sleep. She had to end the misery of being scared all the time, fearful the truth would come out, afraid she would lose her job and even end up in prison.

'Tony,' she murmured softly, 'There's something I want you to do.'

19

It was a day off from work. With Lincoln's death, the case Kari had been covering was finished ... as far as the *Sentinel* was concerned. Her blackmail theory had no legs, no facts, no credibility. Lacking the support of a judge, there were few grounds available for investigating a sitting DA. There was nothing left for Kari to do.

Setting her suspicions and job aside, Kari decided to enjoy the warm spring weather and take Jason for a scenic drive. Her car had a new windshield and a couple patches over the bullet holes in the passenger side seat, but it had a full tank of gas and was running fine.

The journey began with their driving to Provo, some thirty minutes south of West Jordan, then picking up Highway 189, which followed the Provo River up the canyon. There was still snow along the higher mountains, so the river was cloudy and the banks swollen from the melting snow. However the mountain terrain was covered with trees and endless flora, giving way in places to high rocky walls and wide ravines to either side of the road. Their tour continued as far as Heber, Utah, then returned via Deer Creek reservoir which, Kari informed him, was a favorite fishing spot for her father as a child.

It was a pleasant day, the sun was shining and they had ample time to talk. One topic they avoided was the fact that Jason would soon return to England. This day was to be enjoyed, simply a sharing of their lives together. Along the route they stopped at different overlooks or scenic pull-offs, had lunch at a Burger King, and were back in the valley before rush hour traffic hit the main arteries.

'You're an excellent guide and hostess.' Jason praised Kari as she pulled her car into her apartment parking stall. 'I should enjoy visiting that other place you mentioned — Timpanogos Cave, the one with — what did you call them — Helictites and speleothems?'

Kari laughed, as his pronunciation was completely wrong on both words. 'I worked as a tour guide at the cave one summer, when I was paying my way through college. We'll make that visit a priority for a summer trip, when we can drive the Alpine Loop. It's even more beautiful than Provo Canyon, but it's closed during the winter months.'

'I wonder if . . . ' But Jason became aware

of three men. They suddenly appeared spilling out of a black SUV with darkly tinted windows. It had been parked in the visitors' lot, where they could watch for Kari's return.

'Get down!' he shouted.

Kari, shocked by the harsh command, failed to react. Jason grabbed her by the upper arm, yanked her off the seat and pushed her down on the floorboards. Still confused at his surreal behavior, she covered her head with her hands and crouched as low as she could. Jason pulled his gun from the shoulder holster and ducked down on the seat.

Even as he reached for the door handle bullets began striking the car, shattering the back and side windows. Slugs tore through the seat cushions and were embedded into the dashboard. There was a spray of flying glass and the thuds of bullets ripping through metal all around them. One round singed Jason's flesh as it tore a path through the jacket at the top of his shoulder.

The three men continued firing their semi-automatic rifles as they approached — one man to either side and one directly behind. Jason surmised they would continue shooting and keep him and Kari pinned down until they surrounded the car. Once they were even with the front doors, it would mean death for him and Kari both.

Desperate to save their lives, Jason risked lifting his head up enough to glance into the side mirror. He spied the gunman approaching on the passenger side of the car. The shooter paused momentarily, having run out of ammunition from what appeared to be an M-19 assault rifle. He hurriedly removed one clip and began to reload with a second ammo clip. Taking advantage of his being preoccupied, Jason threw open the passenger door, leaned out and took aim. A single shot knocked that attacker to his knees. It also caused the other two to halt their approach. Obviously, they had not expected anyone to shoot back at them. Their surprise gave Jason time to reverse his body's direction and reach the broken window on the driver's side.

With a hasty glimpse over the seat cushion, he saw that the gunman from directly behind the car had moved over to help his fallen cohort. The third man wavered, as he had stopped to check on his two companions. It was the last look he got. Jason quickly aimed out the window and put a bullet into his chest. The impact of the slug drove him backward and off his feet.

With only one able attacker remaining.

Jason scrambled out of the car, using the side of the car and its rear fender for cover.

The gunman sprawled on the ground appeared lifeless, with his arms flung out to either side. The other two were trying to make it back to the SUV. They both had their backs to Jason as he popped up from his hiding place.

'Hold on!' Jason shouted, taking several quick steps in their direction, his gun ready to fire instantly. 'Drop your weapons or die where you stand!'

The injured man had already lost his rifle. The other, being caught in an undefendable position, had no alternative but to surrender. He cursed their bad luck and let his gun fall to the ground. Although he had one arm around his wounded comrade, he raised his other hand in the air.

'Kari!' Jason shouted over his shoulder, fearful she might have been hit. 'Are you all right?'

'Jason?' Kari's voice was uncertain, but she crawled out of the bullet-riddled car. She was visibly shaken, but appeared unharmed.

'Call for help,' Jason told her. 'I'll keep watch over these three.' Kari dug out her cell phone and dialed 911. Once the police were on their way, she contacted Grady.

Grady and Hampton were at Kari's apartment. The police had taken away the three shooters and their SUV. Several uniforms had been posted to watch the complex and were checking IDs of anyone going or coming.

'The one you killed was Mike Sirocco,' Hampton reported to Jason and Kari, who were sitting together on the sofa. 'The other two were brothers — Chico and Felix Rojas. All three had phony California IDs.' He gravely added: 'And all three have outstanding warrants and are known to have worked with the Colombian cartel.'

'Why would they target us?' Kari asked. 'I haven't learned anything of value concerning the drugs in this valley.'

'Rumor has it that you have,' Grady told her. 'I spoke to Rick Cory a few minutes ago on the phone. He said he had just heard about a contract being put out on you from Radar. The word on the street is you have located a source who knows the inner workings of the cartel.'

'So they sent a hit team,' Hampton stated. 'These three men were contract killers, professionals. I doubt we'll get a word out of either of the brothers. A team of lawyers showed up at the hospital,' he snorted contemptuously, 'while Chico was still in surgery. Those guys will probably do a few years for attempted murder, but they won't talk.'

Kari found solace in having Jason's arm around her shoulders, but even that was not enough to quell her inner terror. 'If they truly believe I know something, they'll be back.'

'We're going to try to back-trace who leaked the information on the street,' Hampton promised. 'Radar told Cory this bit of information had the same feel about it as the tip about Chock Lincoln. It seemed to materialize out of nowhere.'

'You think this information was released by someone not actually connected with the cartel?' Jason asked.

'We don't know,' Hampton admitted. 'This could tie in with Dom and Juno, or it could be that someone thinks you two have discovered something new.'

'We've got to concern ourselves about Miss Underwood's life right now,' Grady told him. 'We need to figure this out, before another team of killers tries to fulfill the contract on her.'

'We're leaving three sector cars here and six uniforms to protect you tonight,' Hampton advised them. 'Tomorrow we'll move you to a safe house.'

Jason patted Kari on the shoulder and rose to his feet. 'I'd like a word in private, Detective Hampton. Do you mind?'

The two of them went into the bedroom, while Grady stood uncomfortably next to the loveseat.

'Are you going to face an inquiry for Jason having a gun?' Kari asked the detective.

'After him being forced to use that very gun to save your lives?' Grady grunted. 'Only an idiot would try and make something out of that. I'm glad he is a good shot.'

Kari laughed, a humorless mirth. 'I didn't see anything of the fight. Jason pushed me down under the dash and I was busy ducking the flying glass. Next thing I know, he's telling me to call the police and he has the shooters in custody.'

Grady grinned. 'Your boyfriend proved he is cool under fire. He only took two shots and hit his target both times.'

'It's all so frightening,' Kari said. 'I can't get it out of my head — those men wanted to kill us both.'

'Everything will be all right.' Grady's voice conveyed his compassion. 'You'll see. We'll have the entire department and every snitch in the city working twenty-four-seven until we figure out who put a contract on you. Then we'll shut them down . . . every dammed one of them!'

Hampton and Jason returned shortly and the pair of detectives left the apartment. Jason and Kari were alone at last.

'I don't think meeting Reggie for dinner is a good idea tonight,' Jason said, displaying a charming smile. 'I'll ring him up and let him know. What do you say to us roughing it a bit and cooking for ourselves?'

'What did you and Detective Hampton talk about?'

'I wanted to outline an idea for him, then make sure he chose a secure location for the safe house.'

'And did you agree on where that should be?'

'I suggested my place in Sutton, but he said the department wouldn't spring for the airline tickets.'

The jest caused her to smile. 'Hard for me to write my story from there, too.'

'The good detective said the location will be a tightly guarded secret. I told him I didn't think you would tell anyone at work. But your friend — Dee? You said she's very intuitive.'

'She ought to be an interrogator for the police,' Kari agreed. 'She knew the very first time we . . . ' she hesitated and finished, 'the

261

first time we were intimate.'

Jason laughed, but grew serious at once. 'One thing the attack settled, I'm not returning home just yet.'

Kari moved over to put her arms around him. 'What a crazy relationship we have. The only way I can keep you here is if my life is in jeopardy!'

★ ★ ★

The next morning was like something from a movie. Kari's vehicle had been towed away the previous night, so three police cars escorted Jason's rental car to a parking garage. From there, Jason and Kari, both wearing protective vests, were ushered to Captain Mercer's office. Grady and Hampton were there as well.

Jason was interviewed first with the three men alone. Then Kari was brought in and sat down next to him.

'Miss Underwood,' the captain began. 'I have to ask, do you have any idea how a hit team from California happened to be waiting at your apartment complex?' At her negative reply, he next wanted to know, 'Is there anything you have learned pertaining to the drug cartel that you haven't told us?'

'Nothing at all,' Kari replied. 'I only did the

one story on the cartel. Like your department, the single case I've been working on lately is the murder of Dom and Juno . . . and that is finished!'

'There is the blackmail angle,' Grady pointed out.

'Yes, but without access to certain records that's pretty much a dead end.'

'The DA was curious as to how a visiting officer from the Sutton CID happened to be carrying a weapon,' the captain advised Jason, 'I told her it was a preventative measure that saved both of your lives. She didn't feel that we would have any trouble defending our action or yours in court.'

'As expected,' Grady interjected, 'we got nothing out of the two perps. Their lawyers were at the hospital almost before they arrived. Neither attorney will admit who called them for their client.'

The captain spoke to Kari again. 'If the drug cartel is after you, we have no choice but to hide you. We have a place in mind where you'll be safe until we figure out who is behind this and why.'

'I really didn't want to go into hiding.'

'We'll put every man on this,' Captain Mercer promised. 'Grady and Hampton will work on this exclusively. We won't give up until we find out who's behind this.'

'Knowing these are very powerful people, they will have eyes and ears everywhere,' Grady warned. 'It means keeping you in a secluded location and not using a phone or email. We'll let your bosses and family know you'll be out of touch for a while. It's best if you don't contact anyone personally. The slightest mistake could lead a second hit team to your door.'

'We've a foolproof plan for moving you,' Hampton said. 'But you need to give us your phones for the time being. We'll provide you with a couple clean ones that can't be tracked for emergencies.'

'Are you going to assign a number of police officers to stay with us?' Kari asked.

'No,' the captain answered. 'Inspector Keane will be your only physical protection. We believe the fewer people involved, the safer the both of you will be.'

'We'll provide enough supplies for a day or two,' Grady said, talking directly to Jason. 'If you need anything, you can call me and I'll see you get it.'

Hampton also gave a meaningful nod to Jason. 'Yeah, this shouldn't take longer than a day or two.'

'Jolly good,' Jason replied.

Kari frowned at the cryptic exchange between him and the detectives. 'What on earth can you learn in a day or two?' she queried. 'We might be locked away in a private prison until we're old and gray!'

'Trust us,' Hampton said. 'This is how it has to be.'

Kari gave Jason a sharp look, but he seemed agreeable to the idea of being confined in a gilded cage. With a sigh, she asked, 'So what's next?'

★ ★ ★

Gloria entered the captain's office and waved her hand at the numerous empty desks out on the main floor.

'Did a fire alarm go off that I didn't hear?' she asked the captain. 'Where is everybody?'

'We have three details out right now, all working together to move Miss Underwood and her British sidekick to a safe house. Two cars are being used as decoys, in case the drug dealers are watching.'

'You really think that's necessary?'

'It was a professional hit team that went after them at Miss Underwood's apartment. If not for the Brit having a gun . . . ' He didn't have to finish.

'Yes,' Gloria sanctioned, 'it was rather unorthodox to arm a foreign police officer, but it proved to be a wise decision.'

'We're moving those two where they won't be found for a few days. Maybe we'll get lucky with the new information Miss Underwood has uncovered.'

Gloria lifted a sculpted eyebrow. 'New information?'

'Keane is pretty sure it will expose the blackmail plot. More importantly, the reporter said she has proof concerning the leader of the cartel.'

'How can that be?'

'Well, it seems Miss Underwood took some notes when she interviewed Juno and Dom. She didn't think the two boys had said anything of interest until this attack on her. Now she is certain the information is in her head. She need only remember some odd slang terms Dom used.'

'Sounds pretty iffy to me.'

'She and Keane are going to sort it all out while they are under our protection.'

Gloria hid the dread that swept through her. 'I certainly hope they come through for us,' she said, taxing her raging emotions to sound enthusiastic. 'It's time we ended the cartel's drug trade and put the death of Judge Westmoreland's son to bed.' Then, after a short pause. 'You're sure about this safe house being secure? Those drug people always seem to know what's going on.'

'We've used the Copeland house a number of times. It's off the beaten track, and sits by itself, among the trees and brush. Being up above Cottonwood Boulevard and mixed in among several mansions, it's the perfect spot for them to hide.'

'Good thinking.' Gloria gave her approval. 'Who would think of looking for anyone up there?'

'Was there something you needed?' Captain Mercer asked. 'I'll have some detectives free shortly.'

'No, I only stopped by for a progress check. I thought Cory might have learned something about the hit team or who hired them.'

'I talked to him earlier and he had nothing. If this is cartel business, that's pretty much par for us ... we always end up with nothing.'

'All right. It seems you have everything under control. I'm charging the Rojas brothers with attempted murder of a police officer ... even though Jason Keane is not a member of our own law enforcement. That will allow a little room for plea bargaining. Facing a death sentence if we convict those two of trying to kill a police officer, they might give up a name or two.'

The captain didn't think so. 'Good luck

with that,' he said. 'Those boys know the system, and their lawyers are specialists at getting deals without giving up any real information.'

'There will be no deals, not for such a savage attack. They will be old men when they eventually take a breath of free air again.'

'Glad to hear it,' the captain said.

She bid him goodbye and left the office. Even before she reached the street she was digging in her purse for her cell phone to make a call.

20

The Copeland house had been seized by the Feds during a drug bust. At one time, the basement had been a lab, used to manufacture a host of amphetamines and barbiturates. Because of it's seclusion and a great deal of caution, it remained in business for years. Now renovated, it was a normal looking house with a yard that had become overgrown with weeds and shrubs. The 'For Sale' sign hanging on a post out front was faded from the weather and was nearly unreadable. Although the location was spectacular, most potential buyers were nervous about buying a house that had previously been a drug lab.

Kari and Jason made a quick inspection of the house and discovered a room in the basement that was not mentioned in the property listing. It was what is known as a panic or safe room. The drug dealer must have been paranoid, as the room was built to withstand almost anything. The steel door could be bolted from the inside and it had reinforced walls and roof, over a thick concrete floor. The room also included an emergency light and hardwired phone. There was a secondary air supply to the room, which was provided by a vent that popped up out among some trees, fifty feet from the house. The piping had been disguised as part of an abandoned water pump.

Grady escorted them through the house and showed them the grounds. Afterwards he took a walk around the outside perimeter while they waited inside, out of sight. Ten minutes later he met them back at the front door.

'What do you think?' he asked.

Kari answered. 'The stove is in working order and we've got plenty of groceries. I didn't see a lot of pots and pans, but we'll make do.'

'We can leave a couple cops here,' Grady offered. 'I don't like the idea of your being on your own.'

'It's only a quarter-mile to the road and we've neighbors on both sides,' Jason replied.

'Neighbors you can't see for the trees,' Grady reminded him. 'These lanes wind around through the forest and there's an acre or more between each home. This housing development was designed back when this was nothing but a wilderness area.'

'We'll be fine,' Jason said. 'We both have the mobiles you provided, I'm armed, and the safe room looks impregnable.'

'All the same, you both keep away from any open windows,' Grady warned them. 'No need taking any chances.'

Kari stood alongside Jason as Grady got into his car, backed around, then drove up the lane and was lost in the trees.

'It smells wonderful here,' Kari said. 'There's still dew on the leaves and the sun is shining. I wish we could take a long walk and enjoy this beautiful spring weather.'

'We had best stay inside and keep an eye out for anyone snooping around,' Jason told her.

'But this is a safe house,' Kari objected. 'No one knows we're here.'

'Not unless we were followed, or if someone figured a way to track us, or if one of the police involved in our protection detail is being paid off by the cartel.'

'You sure know how to kill a mood,' Kari complained.

'Let's just be careful for the first little while. As we learned from yesterday's experience, these drug people play for keeps.'

'OK, I'll see about rustling up some lunch. We only have a six-pack of Pepsi and a gallon of milk. Don't know how long that will last us,'

'You didn't bring any tea?'

Kari giggled. 'Oh, did I forget to mention tea?'

Jason grinned. 'You do us a brew up and I'll check and make sure all of the doors and windows are locked.'

'And keep the curtains closed,' Kari added. 'Remember what Detective Grady said — no enjoying the natural scenery.'

They spent the day watching a little television and enjoying each other's company. Supper was a simple salad and bowl of soup . . . followed by a cup of tea. Then, after the sun disappeared over the Oquirrh mountains to the west, Jason kept watch from a darkened window while Kari washed up the few dishes.

Like any good sentry Jason, a careful man, took notice of the shapes within his vision. When darkness came, he could then pick out each one and recognize any . . .

Jason caught his breath. Was that . . . ? Yes, he caught a glimpse of a shadow that moved quickly between the trees. After a few moments he picked up another form, barely visible amongst the thick brush.

'We've got company!' he warned Kari.

'What?' Kari cried. 'Is it the police?'

'No.' Jason said firmly. 'Get to the stairs. I'll kill the lights and be right behind you.'

Kari stared at him in disbelief. 'How could

they have possibly found us?'

'Get going,' Jason instructed, no longer concerned about the how. He was now concerned about staying alive. 'Call for help, but do it on the way down to the safe room!'

Kari disappeared through the hallway door, quickly making her way downstairs. Jason gave her a few seconds before he reached for the wall switch and shut off the lights. Unfortunately, killing the lights appeared to be a signal for the end of the world!

Gunfire blasted through the windows and blew holes in the front door. Jason dove for cover and crawled the last few feet to the stairway.

A powerful explosion took out part of the front wall and shook the entire foundation. Lunging through the entryway, Jason rolled down the first few steps in his effort to escape being hit by the hail of gunfire. Kari was shouting wildly into the phone as Jason got his feet under him and scrambled down the remaining stairs. He grabbed her by the arm as a second explosion rocked the upstairs. The sounds of men's feet entering the house and a guttural snarling of orders could be heard.

'Get in to the room!' he ordered, practically dragging Kari through the door. Once inside, he slammed the door closed and used the massive deadbolt to lock the attackers out.

'Did you get the police?' Jason asked, feeling along the wall until he located a switch that turned on the single battery-operated light.

'I couldn't get through,' Kari panted, breathless from the terror of being attacked a second time. 'The 911 operator — I tried to tell him, but I lost the connection when you pulled me into the room,'

Jason had his gun drawn, watching the door. He tipped his head toward the emergency phone. 'Try the dedicated line.'

Kari picked it up, but it was dead. 'How can that be?' she cried. 'It worked when we checked it a few hours ago!'

Jason removed his mobile but could not get a signal. 'This is not good.' He stated the obvious. 'They are jamming the signals and have cut the phone line.' He could not hide his concern for their safety. 'The plan — it should have worked. There should have been no danger.'

Someone arrived outside the door. There came a pounding noise and several ineffectual shots were fired at the walls. After a few quiet moments there came a deafening explosion. It shook the building and almost knocked Jason and Kari off of their feet. Dirt particles were shaken from the ceiling, dusting them both, and a small crack appeared in the concrete floor.

'Plan?' Kari coughed from the powdery haze and moved closer to Jason. She stared at him, her complexion pale and eyes wide and frightened in the dim emergency lighting. 'We had a plan?'

'It was designed to catch the party responsible for all of this, the one who was being blackmailed and the one giving information to the cartel!'

'Well,' Kari said, frowning, 'I'd say, at this juncture, the *plan* pretty much sucks!'

'Granted,' Jason agreed. 'This isn't the resolution I had in mind.'

'Open up in there!' a man shouted from the other side. 'You open the door and we'll make this quick. If we have to, we'll find the air vent and pump chlorine gas into it. You'll die choking on your own vomit!'

'We've summoned the police and they're on their way,' Jason called back. 'You are running out of time.'

'Ain't no one coming to help you two,' the man sneered. 'You're both dead!'

* * *

Hampton was about to sit down to a boring and bland TV dinner when the phone rang.

He answered and it was Peggy, the dispatcher from work.

'Hey there, angel face,' he cooed the words. 'I was just thinking how I wished you weren't on the night shift. My cooking — '

'Something is wrong!' Peggy cut him off. 'I asked Emergency Dispatch to let me know if any calls came in from . . . well, you know where.'

'And?' Hampton was deadly serious now. He had given Peggy a heads-up about the safe house, without actually mentioning the address. She knew the area and was monitoring it for him.

'The call was choppy and the operator lost it, but I'm certain it was your reporter friend. I listened to the tape and she identified herself . . . right before there was a loud crash and the call went to static.'

'Thanks, beautiful. I owe you!'

'What do you want me to do?'

'Send every sector car you've got to Mountain Meadow Vista Road . . . the old Copeland house!'

'On their way!' Peggy responded . . . and she was gone off of the line.

Hampton grabbed his gun, jacket and car keys, leaving his meal sitting on the table. He hit the button on his cell and phoned Grady on his way to the car.

'Ham?' Grady wondered. 'What's up?'

'Underwood and the Brit are under attack!'

Grady swore . . . immediately adding 'Sorry, Kitten,' for doing it in front of the kids. Then he came back to Hampton. 'But we had it covered. How could this . . . ?'

'I'm at my car and heading up there. You'd better get moving too!'

'On my way.'

★   ★   ★

There was no cover inside the safe room. It had not been foreseen that the occupant might have to defend himself with the door open. Now, that seemed a distinct possibility. Jason moved the table, chair and single cot to form a barricade. Unfortunately, there was nothing solid enough to stop bullets.

'Bollocks!' Jason growled as they couched behind the inadequate cover. 'Someone was one step ahead of us!'

Kari trembled and clung to his arm. 'I thought this was a ploy to trap the blackmailer?'

'Regrettably, the drug cartel must have missed that part of the news brief.'

Several hard bangs came at the door. It sounded as if it was being struck with something heavy. Thankfully, it continued to hold.

'Maybe they are out of explosives,' Kari whispered to Jason.

'Last chance!' an angry voice bellowed from the hallway beyond the door. 'If we have to cut our way through, that little reporter is going to wish you had let us put a bullet in her head. A few of my friends here have a special treat in mind for her!'

Jason called back, 'The police are on their way. If you want to remain a free man, you should leave right now.'

That elicited another vicious oath. 'You've had your chance! Now you're both going to die . . . real slow!'

A piercing stream of bright light suddenly flared between the door and its frame. They were attempting to cut through the bolt with a blowtorch. Time was short.

Jason turned to Kari and his heart yearned for a way to save her life. Facing a no-chance situation, he had her look at the gun.

'I will hold them back as long as I can. If I go down, you grab the gun, stick the barrel under your chin, lean your head forward and pull the trigger.'

Kari's eyes were wide with terror, yet the tears were not for fear of dying, but regret at losing a chance of true happiness. 'I love you,

Jason,' she murmured softly. 'I pray God will grant that we may be together after death.'

Jason ached to kiss her one last time, but the cutting torch was nearly through the locking mechanism. He raised the gun and aimed at the door. Any second now, their lives would end . . . violently!

21

'Quiet!' someone hollered on the opposite side of the door and the torch was suddenly extinguished. The abrupt total silence caused Jason's ears to ache from the strain of listening. Through the numbing quietude it sounded like . . .

'Cops!' came a cry from farther away, possibly the top of the stairs.

There was more cursing, the sound of sirens approaching, and the clamor of footsteps running up the stairway. Jason rose to his feet and turned toward Kari . . . just in time to catch her. She threw herself into his arms and smothered him in kisses. He returned her ardor and their kiss became fused with their combined relief and passion. It was the most immobilizing, unrestrained embrace he had ever received in his life. Had he not been forced to hold Kari up — due to her feet not touching the floor — he would have sunk to his knees in complete elation.

★ ★ ★

Kari, Jason, Grady and Hampton were in Captain Mercer's office. The captain was more than a little repentant about the attack on the safe house.

'We thought we had every angle covered,' he explained. 'We arrested a chain of four people before the attack took place. There should have been no danger.'

'You'll excuse me for pointing it out,' Kari didn't hide her annoyance, 'but it didn't turn out that way!'

'Come with me,' the captain said, gesturing to the door. 'As you both nearly lost your lives, I'll allow for you to witness exactly what happens next.'

Kari and Jason trailed along behind the captain. He opened a door that led to an observation room. On the opposite side of a large window sat a familiar redheaded woman — District Attorney Gloria Streisand. Her controlled wrath was visible within her haggard, yet anxious, expression.

Grady and Hampton had not joined them to observe, but appeared instead at the interview-room door. They bid the uniform cop who had been keeping Gloria company to leave.

'I don't know what you people think you're doing.' Gloria immediately attacked the two detectives vehemently, 'But I'll have your jobs for this! I'll have you all up on charges!'

'You were read your rights?' Grady asked politely, ignoring her threat.

Rather than answer the question, she shouted: 'You've held me against my will the whole dammed night! I demand you tell me what this is about!'

'DDA Martin has confessed everything to us,' Grady informed her.

As Gloria tried to process that mentally, Hampton motioned to someone outside in the hallway. Don Streisand appeared and shuffled into the room. He stopped as he reached the table and regarded his wife with a sorrowful countenance.

'Don?' Gloria was shocked. 'What are you doing here?'

'These detectives came to see me yesterday,' Don replied. 'I had to tell them the truth.'

'Truth?' Gloria was dumbfounded. 'What truth?'

'I'm the one who took pictures of you and Tony Martin,' Don admitted. 'I knew you were cheating on me. I . . . ' He lowered his head shamefully. 'I thought, if you were caught — blackmailed by someone — you would break it off with Tony. I tried to show you that I still loved you, but you kept pushing me away.'

'That's why you were being especially nice and we had the night out at Flemming's,' Gloria muttered inanely. Then she glowered at him. 'You mean to tell me that you took pictures of me and Tony, then extorted fifty thousand dollars from me, all to try and save our marriage?'

'I didn't know you suspected Dominick until you mentioned that he and Juno might have been involved in blackmail. After that . . . ?' He shrugged his shoulders. 'I was afraid you'd hire someone to kill me too.'

Gloria sprang up from her chair defiantly. 'I absolutely, positively, did not order those boys killed! That moron, Chock Lincoln, was only supposed to get the pictures back and scare Dom into silence. Then he upped and killed Hector Gomez to cover his stupidity and make this look gang-related. It was all him!'

Grady cleared his throat before intruding into their conversation. 'DDA Martin, in a plea for leniency, told us how you ordered him to put the word out on the street as to where Lincoln was hiding. He also admitted to planting the guns and computer — which Lincoln had turned over to him — in the man's room.'

'Lincoln was guilty of three murders; he

paid the price for his crimes,' Gloria avowed. 'It was justice.'

'What about Miss Underwood?' Grady jeered. 'You sent him after her too.'

'He was only to warn her off, make it appear as if this was all about drugs and the Colombian Cartel.'

'And the hit teams?' Hampton charged, his voice thick with anger. 'Were they only supposed to warn her and the Brit?'

Gloria closed her mouth and sat down. Don scrutinized her with incredulity. 'All of this because you wanted out of our marriage.' He heaved a sigh. 'You only had to be honest with me, tell me it was over.'

Gloria swallowed hard and looked at him with tear-filled eyes. 'I didn't mean for any of this to happen.'

'So,' Grady's face was red from controlling his rage, 'having DDA Martin spread word on the streets that Kari knew the identity of the drug kingpin, then providing the address of the safe house for the cartel hit squad — those were simply unhappy quirks of fate?'

Gloria blinked back her tears and stubbornly grit her teeth. 'I am invoking my right to counsel.'

Captain Mercer led Jason and Kari back to his office. After a few minutes they were joined by Grady and Hampton. Once the door was closed Kari was the first to speak.

'All of this trouble, caused by a woman over committing adultery.'

'The confession of DDA Martin and the admission from DA Streisand doesn't account for the attack at the safe house,' Jason said. 'What went wrong with the plan?'

'We thought we had every contingency covered,' Hampton was the one to reply.

'Everything worked to perfection.'

'Pray tell what went wrong,' Jason requested.

'Yes,' Kari was quick to join him. 'We were about one second away from dying. That doesn't sound like a foolproof plan to me.'

'Each step went as expected . . . until the attack,' Hampton admitted. 'After Jason decrypted your notes, we figured we knew who was being blackmailed. The plan was to bring everyone out in the open and arrest them red-handed. The cartel should have never been a part of this.'

At Kari's perplexed frown, Jason cleared his throat. 'Better start from the beginning.'

Hampton sighed and started again, speaking to Kari. 'Jason showed me your notes and explained Rick Cory's help with some of the slang. We deciphered the meaning of the sentences you jotted down from when you met with Juno and Dom.'

Jason took over. 'The term *hitting it*, meant Gloria was engaging in a romantic tryst with another person. The *getting baked* was only a slang term for using drugs, so it didn't figure into the blackmail. However, calling Gloria's lover a *fizzle* indicated DDA Martin, who was obviously her amorous lackey. It's exactly what the woman was afraid you had learned at Dom and Juno's house.'

'So Gloria and DDA Martin got Chock Lincoln off on a weapon's possession charge,' Kari concluded. 'Then she sent him after Dom and Juno.'

'You heard her admit that much of the story,' Captain Mercer said. 'And when Gloria thought you were about to uncover her part in all of this, she had Martin put news on the street that you knew who was behind the drug cartel.'

'Getting back to the plan,' Jason took over, 'Captain Mercer told Gloria where the safe house was to get her to act. As soon as she passed the information to DDA Martin, she was nicked and confined without any outside contact. The same went for Martin, once he had given the information to a street informant named Selene.'

'Selene was picked up as soon as she spoke to Radar.' The captain assumed the explanation. 'Radar was nabbed, but not before he

286

managed to make a phone call. We checked the call but weren't too concerned because he had contacted Rick Cory.'

'So who ordered the attack on us?' Kari asked.

Rather than answer the question, the captain said, 'The information I gave Gloria was that you could not only solve the blackmail, but that you had discovered who was working with the Colombian cartel.' Captain Mercer lowered his head. 'We knew she would have to act fast and she did.'

'You claim to have arrested everyone who knew where we were,' Kari said. 'If that's true, who gave away our location?'

'We didn't arrest Rick Cory,' Hampton told her. Then with a sad shake of his head, 'Because we didn't know that he and Radar were working with the drug cartel.'

Kari gasped in shock. 'Not Rick! He wouldn't do that!'

The captain presented a look of disgust. 'We checked the call history on both his and Radar's cell phones. The day Chock Lincoln died, Radar's first call was to Rick Cory. Rick then called both Jesse Ventura and Victor Orozco. He alerted them a full two hours before the attack at the motel, meaning Rick gave the address to the two gang leaders.'

'He might have justified his actions by

claiming he was allowing the Hard Corps and the Lobos to have their revenge,' Kari suggested. 'It might have been a way to stop any other violence.'

'The night you were attacked outside your apartment,' said Captain Mercer, not addressing her comment, 'Radar's phone showed only one call that entire afternoon . . . to Rick Cory. He is the one who passed along the information to a blocked number — we think someone working for the cartel. A few hours later and you had three gunmen blasting away at your car.'

Jason put a consoling hand on Kari's arm. 'I'm sorry, love, but the evidence is very much against him.'

'He's in the lockup downstairs,' the captain told her. 'When I spoke to him, he defended his actions by saying he was saving lives. When Cory took over the gang unit there were a dozen shootings every week. Many of those wounded or killed were innocent bystanders and the streets weren't safe to walk. He brought order to the drug trade and eliminated most of the infighting. If anyone got out of line, he would use his position in the gang unit to find a way to take them down.'

'I can't believe he ordered us killed,' Kari murmured, still suffering shock from the deadly betrayal.

'He believed Gloria was telling the truth about what you knew. The information came from the DA herself. Cory had to tell the Colombians to protect himself, and they sent the hit squads.'

Hampton summarized: 'Having failed in their first attempt, they were only waiting to discover your location. Gloria provided that, but we had no idea Rick Cory was involved.'

Kari sniped, 'That man just got crossed off of my Christmas-card list!'

'And that's about all there is,' Captain Mercer said. 'I can't tell you how sorry we are that we didn't adequately protect you. We thought we had arrested everyone involved.'

Jason said, 'It also explains how they knew to bring explosives and cut the landline to the telephone in the safe room. The hit team was very well informed.'

Kari frowned at Jason, 'When did you learn the blackmailer was Don Streisand?'

'Remember the wording of the note. Once we decided it wasn't Paul Hanson or Dominick, it had to be Gloria's husband or the secretary,' Jason reported.

'Don had the greater motive and the most to gain,' Hampton added. 'If she divorced him he would probably have been left penniless.'

Grady added: 'And he had been to her office a great many times . . . including back when Gloria occupied the same room as DDA Martin has now.'

The frown remained. 'You might have told me,' she scolded Jason. 'I thought we were partners.'

'It was my idea to keep it from you,' Hampton took the blame. 'I asked him not to say anything, in case the plan didn't work.'

Kari accepted his explanation and returned to quiz the captain, 'What will happen now?'

'Selene will testify and probably get probation. Gloria and Martin will face conspiracy to commit murder and several other charges. As for Radar and Cory, they face attempted murder and drug trafficking. All four of them are headed for long stays at the state pen.'

'It's a funny thing,' Grady said. 'Judge Westmoreland said that his son's death was *one murder too many*.' He bobbed his head at Kari. 'Turns out, it wasn't Dominick's death, but yours, Miss Underwood. You were the one murder too many. In attempting to get to you, everyone involved in murder, blackmail or with the cartel, ended up behind bars or dead.'

Jason's last night in the valley had consisted of dinner out with Reggie, his aunt Sally and Kari. The conversation had been light, other than for Sally asking how it had felt being locked in a panic room and actually being in a panic. After the meal, Jason and Kari had returned to her apartment and spent a final night together.

Now, as Kari sat next to Jason in the airport terminal, she hated each minute that ticked away on the clock, knowing each passing second brought them closer to a long separation. Tears welled up in her eyes and she ducked her head.

'I promised myself I wouldn't cry.'

'Me too,' he replied. 'It's so unmanly.'

The statement caused Kari to laugh. 'Yes,' she sniffed at her tears. 'But I'm about to bawl like a baby.'

Jason grinned. 'Being a proper Englishman, I am bound by my heritage to display a more equable demeanor.'

Kari smiled at his amusing effort. 'I'll have some vacation time built up in about four months,' she told him gently. 'If you don't mind tending after a Yank, I'd love to come visit.'

Jason studied her for a long moment,

drinking in her every feature, dreading the thought of leaving her again. He reached into his pocket and removed a small case.

'Kari, I want you to know how special you are to me,' he began. 'With our current situations, there is little hope we can be together for more than a few weeks during the year.' He took a deep breath and let it out slowly. 'Even so, I wanted to give you something.'

Kari took the small case and opened it. She gasped in surprise, seeing a gold ring with a teardrop diamond setting.

'An engagement ring?' She was breathless. 'Are you asking me to marry you?'

'I'm offering you this ring as a testament of my love for you,' he replied carefully, avoiding any binding obligation. 'If you wish to accept it as an engagement ring, I give it to you as one. If you prefer it to only be a token of devotion, I can live with that too.'

Kari leaned over and kissed him soundly. When she pulled back her eyes were brightly misted with tears.

'I accept this as your proposal, Jason,' she murmured tenderly. 'Although we will be separated by an ocean, I want to be your only love from this day forward.'

'Then I'm asking you to marry me.'

'Yes, I want to marry you,' she said softly.

'Even though I know it might be a very long engagement.'

He removed the ring from the case and slipped it on to the appropriate finger. 'With this ring, I promise you my heart and my love,' he vowed.

Kari was equally sincere. 'Accepting your ring, I promise you my heart and all my love forever.'

Jason kissed her and rose to his feet. 'I must pass through security and find the appropriate gate or I'll miss my flight.'

'Call me once you get home, so I know you made it all right.'

With a final squeezing of her hand, Jason turned away and entered the security station. He took time to wave and snap one more mental photograph of Kari to store in his memory. Then he pivoted about and hurried towards his assigned gate. London was a dozen hours away.

We do hope that you have enjoyed reading this large print book.

Did you know that all of our titles are available for purchase?

We publish a wide range of high quality large print books including:
Romances, Mysteries, Classics
General Fiction
Non Fiction and Westerns

Special interest titles available in large print are:
The Little Oxford Dictionary
Music Book
Song Book
Hymn Book
Service Book

Also available from us courtesy of Oxford University Press:
Young Readers' Dictionary
(large print edition)
Young Readers' Thesaurus
(large print edition)

For further information or a free brochure, please contact us at:
Ulverscroft Large Print Books Ltd.,
The Green, Bradgate Road, Anstey,
Leicester, LE7 7FU, England.
Tel: (00 44) 0116 236 4325
Fax: (00 44) 0116 234 0205

PEROXIDE HOMICIDE

Matthew Malekos

When working a night shift at Manchester's inner-city morgue, forensic pathologist Karen Laos finds herself with the body of an unknown male, apparently murdered by a killer she had pursued six years before. Karen reunites with ageing policeman Detective Inspector James Roberts and together they must identify, locate and catch the killer taunting them both. With an appetite for ritualistic murder and an array of alarming and unusual methods, there is a real threat that this killer will elude their grasp and strike again, leaving only mutilated victims in his wake . . .

BLOOD ON THE WALL

Jim Eldridge

Along the line of Hadrian's Wall, someone is murdering people — and taking their heads. Is this ritualistic killing or a revenge mission? Detective Inspector Andreas Georgiou of Carlisle CID is brought back from suspension to investigate, but with an accusation of brutality on his record and a superior officer set on hanging him out to dry, his work will be anything but straightforward. Fighting battles on several fronts, Georgiou slips deep into a web of corruption, extreme right-wing idealism and the shocking realisation that the identity of the serial killer will be hard to discover and even harder to believe . . .

THE SACRIFICE

Mike Uden

When private eye Pamela Andrews and her daughter, Anna, are chosen to investigate a high-profile case concerning the whereabouts of a missing girl, they wonder why. They're hardly household names and no one really expects them to succeed. Then the penny drops — they've just been cast as headline-grabbing eye-candy. With no help from the police and nothing much to work on, it soon becomes a daunting mission. Hunting down an abductor is one thing. Becoming the next victim is quite another . . .

MONEY NEVER SLEEPS

Stella Whitelaw

Fancy Jones, bestselling crime writer, has discovered that someone is trying to kill her . . . When she is invited to lecture at a writers' conference in the Derbyshire Dales, she leaps at the chance to leave London and hopefully escape the threat of her assassin. But events turn sour when a body is found floating in a lake at the conference venue, and bizarre things start happening to Fancy. Suspicion falls on the other delegates — but has her stalker followed her . . . ?